Books by Lewis Warsh

POETRY

The Suicide Rates
Highjacking
Moving Through Air
Dreaming As One
Long Distance
Immediate Surrounding
Today
Blue Heaven
Hives
Methods of Birth Control

AUTOBIOGRAPHY

Part of My History
The Maharajah's Son

FICTION

Agnes & Sally

FICTION COLLECTIVE

AGNES & SALLY

by Lewis Warsh

 NEW YORK

Copyright © 1984 by Lewis Warsh
All rights reserved.

First Edition

Library of Congress Cataloging in Publication Data

Warsh, Lewis:
  Agnes & Sally.

  I. Title. II. Title: Agnes and Sally.
PS3573.A782A7   1984   813'.54   83-16543
ISBN 0-914590-80-4
ISBN 0-914590-81-2 (pbk.)

Part of this book originally appeared in *Mag City*. Thanks to Gary Lenhart, Greg Masters and Michael Scholnick. And to Bill Corbett.

Published by the Fiction Collective with assistance from the National Endowment for the Arts and the New York State Council on the Arts.

Grateful acknowledgement is also made for the support of Brooklyn College and Teachers & Writers Collaborative.

Typeset by Open Studio, Ltd., in Rhinebeck, New York, a non-profit facility for writers, artists and independent literary publishers, supported in part by grants from the New York State Council on the Arts.

Manufactured in the United States of America.

Text design: McPherson & Company
Cover design: Louise Hamlin
Author photograph: Lorna Smedman

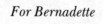

For Bernadette

SALLY SAT AT THE KITCHEN TABLE writing a letter to her friend Agnes. Can I visit? she wanted to know. Is it a good time? She didn't want to sound desperate, but she knew that Agnes thought she was desperate and maybe making her think she truly needed, desperately, to get away, was the best way to be certain Agnes responded affirmatively to her request. She envied her friend her independence (Agnes had gone off to school in Boston, married and moved to New York), for loving her husband (so Sally assumed from a distance), and took pains to choose only words that would veil her real feelings. All Agnes needs, she reasoned, is a glimpse of the person (me) who was once her closest friend, even if that person (me again) no longer exists.

It was the first week of spring and the big elm in the front yard cast its shade over the side of the house, spring was her favorite time of year ("why leave now, you know how much you like it when the weather changes," she could hear her husband say when she told him her plan), but there was more to life than just watching and observing the minutiae of nature: there were people too—isn't that what Agnes always reminded her?—people outside the small town setting where she'd lived all her life, people with things on their minds other than whether there were enough funds for Friday night bingo at the Town Hall or whether Sergeant Hassler, the local police chief, had hired an assistant (I'm quoting a recent article in the local paper), and that's what New York meant: so many people swirling around you you never had to think of any one person separately, just compare them all—some were like hornets, others resembled butterflies or snakes—and take your pick. You didn't have to say hello or nod to each person on the street just because you and the other person were both on the same side of the street at the same time, watching one another as you approached from a distance, then squinting as if to say "don't I know you? haven't we met before?" She wished she could be blunt and tell Agnes what she was really feeling—that most of all she wanted to get away from Bob—but knowing how much Agnes had disapproved of their marriage (not even driving up from Boston for the wedding as a kind of protest against what she thought of as total stupidity on her friend's part) made her look forward to the time they'd actually be sitting together across the dining room table in Agnes's apartment, in the alcove where Agnes and her husband ate and which Sally tried to imagine as she wrote the letter—legs propped on chairs smoking cigarettes and drinking coffee as the afternoon light waned and a breeze blew the curtains up into the room: "It feels more like Huntington here than New York," Sally said when the phone rang: "It's Jake, he's not coming home for dinner."

She'd been to New York with her parents when she was a young girl and with Bob, once, right after they were married, but never alone. ("Why leave now?" meaning "ever" she could hear him say.) She and Bob had stayed over two nights in a hotel near Times Square. They'd spent their first night in the city wandering up and down Broadway, from the door of the hotel to Columbus Circle where Bob—who'd heard about the dangers of Central Park at night—insisted they turn back. On their second night they took a cab downtown to a small theatre near Washington Square to see a performance of *The Ghost Sonata* by Strindberg. They were using some of the money that Sally had inherited when her father died to finance the trip so Bob, who didn't like the theatre, allowed his new wife her pleasures: didn't show any annoyance or signs of impatience—just sat back, when the houselights dimmed, and closed his eyes. When they stood on the street after the play, not sure how to get back to the hotel (all you have to do is call a cab and tell the driver where you're going), Sally felt burdened by the weight of the freedom of being some place new, the demands of the natural exultation she was feeling just being there coupled with the potential excitement of city life, and saw Bob as her protector (albeit he was slightly drunk: Jim Beam in the flask in his jacket pocket), and Huntington a place to go—her home. The truth presented itself as a series of facts: you couldn't see the stars above the rooftops, couldn't go to the park—not even during the day (Bob liked to exaggerate), couldn't sleep at night—a subway rumbled beneath their bed, the walls were paper thin and whoever was staying in the room above paced the floor wearing hiking boots—every step and the ceiling vibrated, men leered out at you from doorways, women with bare shoulders and legs accosted the man you were with—ignored you, stared right through you, as if you weren't there! Though marrying Bob had been the first step, it had informed her only that she wanted to change her life in a manner more complicated than she'd previously determined. Light as air, she had seen the real possibility of making an escape *with* her husband, convinced that she needed someone else—anyone, if only to run interference—more than she needed someone she loved. But Bob had no desire to go anywhere; he liked his life in Huntington. He would go to New York or Boston for a weekend with his wife if that's what she wanted to do and sip whiskey in the men's room even if it meant being around alot of queers! After that trip to New York Sally realized that she could sink into her life in Huntington, go as deep as she wanted without wondering—except when Agnes admonished her—whether he'd made the right move.

The diner which Bob had inherited from his father, and where they both worked, was a place to go, a destination.

Before entering Sally kissed the envelope containing the letter she'd written to Agnes (two handwritten pages) for good luck before dropping it into the blue and red box outside the post office. The body moves along its accustomed track but the thoughts take off in a hundred different directions. There was Pete, the gas station attendant, under his Amoco sign, waving to her from across the street as she walked by (if she didn't walk by, swinging her arms at her sides, would he think something was wrong? Will this town fall apart without me?) There was the row of houses, the fences and yards, and the stump of the tree on the corner, the maple that had died last year, the private houses on the edge of the shopping district which had yet to be replaced by an underground mall and which was her destination: gas station, bank, hardware, grocery, beauty parlor, another grocery, jeweler, insurance agency. Diner. She'd lived in one of those houses for seventeen years; then her parents—first her mother—had died while she was still in highschool and she'd moved in with her aunt who lived on the other side of town, her mother's sister Josephine who was still alive but whom Sally rarely saw or wanted to see—she had married Bob so quickly after her parents had passed away (it was a choice between Aunt Jo and Bob) some people gossiped that she'd married more out of desperation than any real feeling—and it was true: don't make me live with this person anymore. Envy the friend who escapes from home: feel jealousy towards the happily married—even if it's only in one's imagination. People in big cities are no happier than anyone else, they just have more to distract themselves when things go wrong.

"Your car will be ready in a few days," Pete had said, yesterday, when she'd brought it in for a tuneup. But when Bob, later that night, had asked her if anything was wrong with it, she'd been unable to tell him. Then, as usual, he slammed the door after dinner, and she was home again, alone, upstairs in their bedroom, her long nightgown—which she'd discard when the weather grew warmer—tangled between her legs, three pillows beneath her head, *Anna Karenina* balanced on her knees, a glass of water and two pills—not over the counter sleeping pills, but pills which Dr. Amundsen had recently prescribed—on the bedside table.

"In a few minutes he'll be home," she thought, remembering that the car she heard passing couldn't be him, she'd taken the car to Pete's and unless someone drove him from wherever he was he'd have to walk home, and that would make him even angrier than when he left. And when he did come in she'd pretend she was asleep, hear him cursing and stumbling around in the kitchen ("is that you Bob?" she wanted to call out, since if it wasn't—but she refused to pursue that train of thought, it was too easy to imagine something frightening and escape into that feeling which wasn't real: there are enough situations and things that are real and frightening, it's not necessary to invent new ones). Yet the next morning there he was, 8 A.M., in the diner, sweeping up, his 6'6" frame bent almost in half as if he were admiring the scraps of dust circulating in the early morning light pouring through the plate glass windows on which the words PRICE'S DINER had been stencilled in a wide arch—that's where he'd be, and where Sally, after she drank her morning coffee and finished her letter, would follow him, and where they'd spend the day—as if nothing had happened the night before.

"I fell in love with," she wanted to say, "married you," defending herself, "but you're different now."

"I loved him once," she wanted to tell Agnes, who gave her a knowing smile but who had enough sense to sit still and listen and let her ramble on without thinking (she had her own problems) that every other thing she said was a lie.

THOUGH THE TWO GIRLS DIDN'T correspond regularly, they never let more than a few months go by without making an effort of some kind to keep in touch. Most of what Agnes heard about her friend came by way of her mother, not the best source, who still lived in Huntington. As she often did when she received a letter, Agnes began to reply to the person in her head, composing whole sentences without ever writing them down. It might take weeks before she sat down and wrote the letter, her initial inspiration diluted by all the other unwritten responses to letters she'd received in the interval and never answered. Letters like Sally's required an immediate response, but Agnes knew that if she called Sally she might have to talk to Bob, Bob might answer and Agnes couldn't tell from the letter whether Bob even knew about Sally's plan. (If he didn't know, and Agnes called, Bob might think it had been Agnes who had initiated the idea, and that the two old friends were conspiring against him—which is something he thought anyway.) And even if Sally answered Bob might be there, the telephone was in the kitchen, hovering over her, making it impossible to talk intimately. Agnes wished there was a method whereby her thoughts could be translated into messages without her ever having to do anything except stare into space and *think* them. The same with feelings too difficult to describe or put into words. Sally had written

13

poetry for the highschool yearbook, kept a notebook (she still had it) alternating descriptions of things she saw with quotes from the books she was reading. "You have a way with words," her teachers told her, overjoyed at having discovered someone whose interest in books was as genuine, presumably, as theirs had once been. (Or as false: look what happened to them!) Agnes, who had studied acting for three years in Boston before coming to New York, had a way with other people's words, but when it came to dealing with her own felt self-conscious, overcome, as if the manner in which she talked or wrote was more important than what she meant. "You can't help sounding like an actress," Jacob once told her—they were in bed at the time—and writing letters in her head was like memorizing the part in a play, creating dramas out of every minor episode, making a scene for its own sake.

As she contemplated telling Jacob about Sally's plan to visit, knowing he'd be skeptical and attempt to discourage the idea, she began outlining the preliminary stage of the argument she knew would ensue: "If Tony could stay with us"—Tony, Jacob's younger brother, had visited them last year—"why can't Sally?"

There was no question in Agnes's mind that Sally's marriage to Bob Price had been a hideous mistake. High school valedictorian marries high school basketball star. It was a dead end. Agnes had theories about why her friend had given up her chances to go to college in favor of an early marriage, sometimes she wondered why she herself had ever left Huntington, but as time passed it was hard for her to balance logic and empathy and reason with her knowledge of what she imagined her friend was thinking. In her letters, or on the rare occasions they spoke on the phone or saw one another, Sally avoided any mention of Bob or her life in the diner, but tried to encourage Agnes to talk about her life in New York. "Far be it from me to pass judgment on someone else. . . ." If she wasn't going to criticize or analyze what had become of her friend, Agnes could still blame Bob Price, cringe when she thought of him, for allowing and encourag-

14

ing Sally to sink to what Agnes thought of as "his level" (though what she really meant was the low-brow intellectual level of small town life in general). Sally as head of the debating team at Huntington Regional, defending Communist China's right to be admitted to the U.N., Sally quoting the poetry of Ho Chi Minh in World History while Mr. Gamzon and all the other students stared at her in disbelief, Sally sitting crosslegged in the narrow aisle between shelves in the town library (Agnes recalled the time Sally had fallen asleep in the library, only to be discovered, after dark, by Frank Jones, janitor and general handyman for the town buildings: Sally had told everyone except Agnes that she had fallen asleep studying but Agnes knew that she'd fallen asleep purposely so she wouldn't have to go home (she was living with Aunt Jo at the time) and could picture her with her winter coat, a hand me down from Sally's grandmother, cushioning her head from the imitation linoleum squares (the fox fur on the collar of the coat was imitation too): "suddenly I woke up and there he was, standing over me, shining a flashlight in my face—I think he was drunk")—all of Agnes's memories contradicted the image of docile housewife ("and they don't even have any kids!") who worked alongside her husband in that creepy smalltown luncheonette. Back in highschool, Sally's picture had appeared in the local paper as often as Bob's, but for different reasons.

The television, a black and white model with a 12- inch screen which Jacob had bought at a discount at Lechmere Sales in Cambridge, perched on a lopsided mahogany table at the foot of the bed. The sound was off; Jacob, propped against pillows, wearing a T-shirt with Mozart's face looking bereft and amused simultaneously, and dungarees, barefoot, was reading a Nicolas Freeling mystery novel. (Detective Van der Valk had just fallen in love, and now had to tell his wife, Arlette, who was a good cook and Jacob's idea of what every wife should be like: not just a wife, but a comrade, a good friend—that he'd been unfaithful.) Jacob always looked half his age when he read in bed, he might as well be reading an

15

illustrated edition of *Tom Sawyer*, innocent and serious at the same time—lost in his own world which is where, as he often told Agnes, he was happiest. ("Except when I'm with you." Agnes looked insulted and knew he was lying.)

A guest wouldn't interrupt the status quo of this household, or if he or she did—maybe that would be all for the better. Agnes sensed that Sally just wanted to get away from Price's Diner for awhile. Sally had disguised her feelings well, and there was no indication that the idea for the trip had been precipitated by anything stronger than at least a momentary feeling of boredom (it was spring, after all, and Agnes felt a little restless herself), though for her friend's sake Agnes hoped otherwise.

A display counter for prophylactics. Bob Price had screwed all the cheerleaders. Sally had majored in French. She looked French, like a French schoolboy, especially with her hair cut short. She and Agnes had once discussed "going to Europe," going to "E"—it was their code, a way of talking—but that was all in the past, everything the word "had" implied. One could sit back, stare into space, brush one's hair incessantly or compulsively chainsmoke, remember everything one had said or done, every conversation and what one meant to say and didn't, feel regret or bitterness or joy, but there was no escape from the knowledge that one was better off looking ahead—down the road to points unknown—or even better into the present where all one was doing was thinking, oblivious of everything but the sound of traffic in the street below, last rays of sunlight filtering through beige curtains. . . .

"I won't be any trouble," Sally wrote, and Agnes tried to picture her friend, cigarette in hand, at the dining room table of a house Agnes had seen only once, pausing to take a sip from a lukewarm cup of instant coffee, meditative—in a way that Agnes had never been—as she rearranged the thoughts flowing through her head, until they became the phrases and sentences of the letter— which in turn became an entity of its own—Agnes had read. "Sometimes I look around and I want to be somewhere else. It's not that I don't want to be here"—another lie, Agnes thought— "I just want to see other people, other streets, other trees, even. Bob is different, I guess I knew that when I married him, and it's extraordinary to me how he and his father and your mother and all the other people we both know can be content with what seems to be so little—and in judging them I'm judging myself, I know—I'm judging you too but you managed to get away: and I know I'm not the only one, that it's a common problem. Nothing earthshaking—"

Agnes had bought her red leather knee high winter boots at Henri Bendels last December, a belated birthday gift from Jacob who had given her the money, knew how much she wanted them, and figuring that winter was coming on and she needed new boots anyway that she might as well indulge herself—she'd been talking about buying them since she first arrived in New York. Regardless, it was hard for Agnes not to feel guilty about spending all that money, even if it was a gift. In her fantasy she was entering the bedroom through the hallway door, Jacob in bed, reading, but for a moment it wasn't he—at least the features and the color of his hair were different, and she was different too, throwing back her head and laughing as she watched him mark his place in his book, remove his reading glasses with the wire rims ("you look like a French schoolboy," she had said, in approval, as she'd never liked the heavy black frames of the glasses he'd been wearing when they met), make a space for her on the bed. She'd acted out the scene only once when Jacob was at work, standing in front of the empty unmade bed, wearing a blue silk scarf and the boots, modelling herself like an odalisque for a man who wasn't there.

Jacob left for work at eight every morning, returned home at six. Agnes, who was more like Sally than she dared to admit, except that she spent most of her afternoons at home, alone, was in the kitchen.

"Would you like a drink?"

There's an idea of seriousness from which romanticism is

excluded. Growing up in a small town and never leaving might have as much latent romantic significance as growing up in a small town and coming to New York to make your fortune.

Sally dreamed she was in an advertisement for sleeping pills, the kind you can buy over the counter. In every drugstore there was a display of prophylactics under a sign "Family Planning." The girls buy them to give their boyfriends who complain that it dulls the sensation, but they go through with it anyway—in the bedroom of a friend whose parents have gone away for the weekend, or the backseat of a car parked at the end of a country road.

AGNES AND SALLY WEREN'T SISTERS.
When Agnes mentioned that Sally was thinking of visiting, Jacob put up a small argument, unwilling to accept Agnes's comparison between Tony, his brother, and Sally, who may have been Sally's best friend but was still only a friend, and whom Jacob had met twice before and disliked.

Last spring he'd accompanied Agnes to Huntington. There was still snow on the ground, white patches in the sunless areas surrounding the steps of houses and some trees. Agnes's mother had called up a few of her daughter's old highschool friends, but only Sally Price had come for late afternoon coffee and homemade cake in the spacious dining room where Mrs. North ("Oh mother, you shouldn't have bothered!") had taken out her rarely used family china, "French heirlooms" as she described them, for the occasion.

The walls of the dining room and living room were covered with clusters of framed photographs: Agnes, as she appeared in the school play (*Miss Julie*), Agnes and Jacob on their wedding day on the steps of a church in Boston, Agnes's father, Agnes's parents on *their* wedding day (outside the church where Sally and Bob had been married, just down the street), Agnes and her older sister Betsy, Betsy as a baby, Agnes in her highschool graduation gown, Agnes and Sally and a third girl ("that's Susan Amundsen, the doctor's daughter") in bathingsuits at Laurel Lake the summer

19

before their senior years, aunts and uncles Jacob had met at the wedding and from whom they'd received small checks or gift subscriptions or subscriptions to magazines they didn't want or household goods they didn't need like toasters and blenders and hideous electric juicers and can openers and to whom Agnes had written thank you notes which Jacob had signed ("why don't you sign my name for me—wouldn't that be easier?")

While the girls filled in the years that had interrupted their friendship which hadn't been sealed with initials carved in a tree, they hadn't been lovers, after all, just friends, Jacob stared at the first green fringe bordering the front yard of the house which possibly Agnes ("what about Betsy?" "I don't think she'd want to come back *here*") would inherit when her mother passed away, and wondered what it would be like to

Jake and Denise ate lunch together every day for a week, before Denise—who knew he was married—asked Jake over for dinner. It was the night, no coincidence, that Sally was due to visit and Jake realized that if he was going to take a chance and break the rhythm of a life that might just wind along indefinitely with nothing ever happening, not even a ripple from a rock tossed by some stranger on the shore, this was it. They were sitting in a booth in the dark corner of a bar Jake would never have considered eating in alone and when she asked him, out of nervousness perhaps, she flicked the black cigarette lighter she was holding—once, then again, for no apparent purpose—and stared at him over the rim of her drink (a bloody mary), the flick of the lighter like a signal meant for someone else, not Jake, an old lover, perhaps, whom she'd just spotted across the bar. One flick of the lighter meant yes, he's mine. Two flicks: forget it. It was hard to do anything but acquiesce, say "yes," and acknowledge in some unspoken way that he knew she was taking a risk; had made the first move. And now they were riding the elevator together, back to work, no longer as strangers, but with fingers intertwined at their sides. Jake wondered if anyone in the office knew that they were having lunch together (an office was no different from a small town in a lot of ways, everyone knew everything), since many of his co-workers were unmarried and in the few weeks Denise had been working for the company he'd heard talk

live in a small town. He was always talking about ways to make life easier and if nothing else small town life, in comparison to life in New York, had an untrammelled, unclaustrophobic, if boring, air. There was a sense of narrowness which could be translated into simplicity without the feeling of being enclosed or shut in. And you could breathe, freely—that was important. Since taking a few writing courses in college, Jacob had the vague unspoken notion that he would someday like to write a mystery novel, creating a character in the tradition of Maigret, Martin Beck or Van der Valk, his current favorite, but working eight hours a day along with the energy expended just living in New York, just getting around (though most of this energy, he conceded, was mental, thinking about what to do next and whether what he was doing was right), provided him with a perfect

---

about who was going to ask her out first—it was the type of conversation that made Jacob wonder if he was back in highschool or in his college dormitory, and made him realize that marrying young he'd managed to miss the experience of an extended adolescence, or at least the form that the state of being single and free takes when you find yourself at age 23 or 25 or even 30 still doing and thinking the same things you thought about when you were first aware women i.e. "members of the opposite sex" existed. He waited until 5 minutes to 5 before calling Agnes, who didn't seem annoyed or even surprised—though he'd never once, in the past, called to say he was doing "something else" after work, had always come home ("would you like a drink?") at the same time everyday. Yes, Agnes informed him, Sally had arrived safely, and if he wasn't coming home for dinner they'd probably go out to eat together at a local restaurant. He wondered whether she was giving him his freedom to do with as he pleased or if she cared or whether he would have acted similarly, so nonchalant, if it had been she who was calling him. Didn't even ask any questions: who are you going out with (he'd mentioned that he was having dinner with some people at work)? Maybe she thinks I'm being considerate, giving them time to be alone for awhile and talk things over. The phonecall lasted a minute. Agnes's voice sounded hoarse, like it did when he'd first met her and she'd spend all night rehearsing for a play. Denise didn't ask

21

excuse not to do anything but complain inwardly, and then feel guilty, he didn't have time.

Sally's image, in his mind, wasn't a memorable one. Even Agnes had to admit that her old friend "looked terrible." She'd cut her hair again which made her look thinner and taller than she was, in contrast to most small town women who were overweight from inactivity. What was there to do except eat and watch television? Before making the trip, and after Agnes had learned that Sally was planning to visit her at her mother's house, she had briefed Jacob on the high points of that senior year in highschool when the Huntington debating team had gone on to the finals in Manchester, when the basketball team, starring Sally's husband, had lost the state championship in the final game (possibly Sally would bring Bob with her), when Agnes had starred in the class

---

him if he'd called his wife, she was too smart for that. It was as if she were saying: what you do is your business. *I* know you're married, and how I deal with that is my problem. They rode down in the elevator in silence, Denise adjusting the edges of a shawl which she told him she'd bought in a Ukrainian gift shop on First Avenue, but when they reached Fourteenth Street, heading downtown, she took his hand again (who cared who was watching them!) and began telling him what she was planning to make him for dinner and how she didn't know how long she was going to stay at this particular job, it's the first job I found and I was too lazy to look so I took it, the same way with my apartment—it was there, it was available, apartments are hard to come by, at least that's what everyone told me so when I saw this one I just said "yes" and signed the lease. Before taking the job she'd been going to school and living with relatives in Brooklyn. When Jake was going to school in the Bronx he'd often seen the groups of young girls in parochial school uniforms, short blue skirts and white blouses, and wondered if something was wrong with them—at least he sensed that in some way he was different from them—and now he was walking beside one of them listening to her chatter about all the nuns and priests and how her mother would have a heart attack if she knew she was bringing a Jewish boy home to dinner. It had been years since Agnes and he had walked together in public with their arms around each other, though they

play—"that's me in that picture there"—Sally directing—

"I just don't want you to complain about being bored, O.K.?"

Jacob knew the rest. Agnes had gone to Emerson College in Boston to study acting. Sally, whose parents—when they were alive—had discouraged her from thinking about going to college, much to the dismay of her teachers who were certain she could get a scholarship to Wellesley or Holyoke or Smith, had taken her place alongside Bob behind the counter at Price's. Jacob, a junior at Tufts, had met Agnes one misty winter night in the lobby of Symphony Hall, during the intermission of a performance of Brahms' First Symphony. "You leave home, you take a chance, you meet someone—it's that simple." Everyone had a past. Men no longer mind when you tell them you aren't a virgin. Some men like

---

still occasionally held hands, and Jacob couldn't prevent himself from looking back over his shoulder every few moments as if back there on the streets they were leaving behind two people he didn't recognize at first—himself and Agnes—were following them at a discreet distance. And up ahead, there were two other people —Jacob couldn't help but open the door out of the present into the immediate future where the possibility of what could happen when they reached her apartment took the form of a question mark as he turned the pages of the magazine at his desk at work and watched Denise whom he hadn't met yet glide across the floor he unbuttoned her blouse in his mind, but that was later, look at that window (she was pointing to an antique desk, a secretary, in the window of an expensive antique shop), I could use that in my apartment, don't get upset when you see my place (it was four flights up) and I hope you're not allergic to cats (I just moved in remember, and I still need some furniture). Denise lived in a renovated apartment building on 10th Street between 2nd and 1st Avenues, in a neighborhood Jacob and Agnes had ruled out as a possible place to live. As she fumbled in her purse for the key to the downstairs lock Jacob couldn't separate his feelings of nervousness from the euphoria he was somewhat guiltily experiencing. All he wanted was for the voice that said: What am I doing here? to disappear, and happily Denise didn't seem concerned when he didn't say anything for long moments,

older women, rich women in their fifties who spend their afternoons in gyms and saunas. Agnes saw him first: it was she who made the first overture. A simple gesture, a question ("what did you think of the concert?" "I hated it"). Do you have an extra cigarette? May I see your program? Where do you come from? Is this your handkerchief? She wondered what he looked like behind his beard, whether he'd be shocked if they went home together this first night without even really speaking. Home to a dormitory probably, his or mine. Male actors grew beards only to play particular parts, whereas college teachers and male students grew them to fit an image. Would she have to say: do you want me to come home with you? or would he know what she meant—and she hardly considered herself a promiscuous person—without either of them saying anything? They were walking up carpeted steps to the balcony, they were sitting—there'd been a seat vacant on Agnes's right —side by side. When you leave home anything can happen. Your parents don't know

she could chatter endlessly and keep the conversation going as she'd done every afternoon that week over lunch and never give him the impression that she thought he was as boring as he sometimes felt. Boring, in the sense of not being good company. "You live in your head," Agnes said. It made him want to at least attempt to keep up with her, follow the line of thought: if she asked him something about himself he would be inspired to speak! And she did: she wanted to know everything. The only subject that couldn't be discussed was Agnes, not yet anyway. Afterwards, maybe, after they'd been sleeping together for a few weeks, and they'd lie back in the large bed which was big enough not only for Denise and himself but two or three other people if they wanted to join them, smoking Shermans as they listened to the rain and Jake told her how when he'd arrived home that first night he'd found Agnes in bed with that girl, her old friend, Sally, the one I told you about ("you mean she's queer?"), it was something they could laugh about as if the joke were on them.

"I didn't know your wore glasses."

"Oh, sometimes. Do you like them?"

Denise let him open her blouse, then pulled away. Dinner could

24

whether you got drunk, how late you stayed out, or who you slept with. When Agnes learned that Sally and Bob were getting married she didn't go home for the wedding. She thought that her absence would be noticed, but Sally—who was just going through the motions, and hadn't expected her friend to come—didn't care.

On New Year's Eve, sex is always a possible replacement for Guy Lombardo, even if you're fifteen and frightened of going into the local drugstore for a package of "Ramses."

Hidden streams and waterfalls beneath the leaves. . . . Agnes wanted to take Jacob on a tour of Huntington. The snow was definitely melting and with Sally walking between them on the narrow sidewalk they headed through the April sunlight to the center of town.

"There's Bob! There's Bob!" Agnes shouted as they entered the diner, where an old man she didn't recognize as Bob's father ("Old Man Price") sat at the counter, the only customer, drinking a cup of black coffee.

---

wait. "I'll be back in a moment." There were framed photographs on the wall of the apartment facing the bed: Denise in her first communion gown with a small cross at the nape of her neck, Denise and her mother and father ("they died when I was in highschool"), a brother, a best friend—he lay back with his arms beneath his head, head on pillow, and waited, staring up at the ceiling. "Would you like a drink?" and when he didn't answer: "What's wrong?" Here, they'd been living together only a few weeks and already they were fighting, arguing about finding a larger place, Denise wanted to get married and have kids and they hadn't even been introduced, it was lunch hour and they were riding up in the elevator together: I noticed you the first day at work, she said, but did she say it before or afterwards or during, he couldn't remember. The men in the window were putting clothes on a mannikin. "Let's get some wine," she said, a glass of wine with a single icecube. She tossed the bathrobe over the back of a chair, took a sip of wine, and knelt between his legs, unbuttoning his trousers and slipping them down around his ankles. There, then, that is, would be, have. From what it would be, the way it goes. Athena was born from the head of Zeus. You can buy magazines like this on newsstands everywhere.

25

In the days when they were all in highschool together, Agnes and Bob had been anything but close friends. In fact, when Sally had written Agnes in Boston about her marriage plans Agnes had replied, bluntly, that she'd never in a million years accept the idea that she (Sally) could ever be happy with anyone so stupid . . . so insensitive . . . as Bob ("The Moper" as they called him) Price.

It's not hard to get into people's minds, to understand what they're thinking at any given moment. Most people reveal their thoughts by means of facial expressions and gestures; in most cases it's best just to ignore whatever they say.

Jacob recalled the sloping shoulders of the man called "Bob," who without smiling extended his hand, detaching it from his body as he leaned across the counter to meet his wife's former best friend's husband. Sally hadn't told him she was going to see Agnes, much less warned him they would possibly all end up meeting on opposite sides of the counter in a shabby diner in the middle of nowhere.

The thigh muscles of a basketball star. . . . When they first married, Bob used to wake an hour before he was due at the diner and run in the early morning light down Main Street, to the ballfield, around the bases, and if he felt ambitious to the cemetery (where Sally's parents, and Bob's mother, and Agnes's father were all buried) on the outskirts of town. Now he slept as late as possible, and when the alarm went off pushed out with that massive right arm pulling the covers from around the woman sleeping beside him, who, in his dreams, had been replaced by an Indian girl in braids who'd been raped by white hunters or Elke Sommers in a low cut gown with a slit up the side whom he'd seen the night before as a guest on The Tonight Show.

The two men shook hands. It wasn't momentous, nor a signal of camaraderie, as when two members of opposing teams shake hands publicly before a game.

Agnes (in her red boots) in front of the bathroom mirror.

WHEN BABS LAROSA TOLD HER
mother she was pregnant, Connie—whose husband had left
her when Babs was five—offered to bring up the baby herself,
"under my own roof," and "if needs be," she told her daughter, rising to the dramatic spirit of the situation, "with my
own hands." She had little confidence that her daughter, at
twenty, had the patience or discipline or interest to spend the
next ten years (at least) of her life devoting herself to taking
care of a child, and it was only after she'd fully developed the
scene in her mind, imagining all the paraphernalia necessary
to taking care of a baby (what the Welfare Department calls a
"layette"): the crib, the crib sheets, the rubber sheets, the crib
mattress, the playpen, the stroller, the basinette, the high-
chair, the diapers (there was a diaper service two towns over),
rubber pants, diaper pins, diaper pail, all the little sleeping
suits and tights and undershirts—that she thought to ask her
daughter about the father: who was he, "who is he!" and
whether he accepted responsibility, did he even know? Is he a
local boy? She thought of Eddie White, who used to work at
the gas station, and whom Connie had once seen walking
with Babs arm in arm down Main Street, but in the years
since she'd left highschool Connie had lost track of her
daughter's boyfriends, and Babs hadn't mentioned Eddie
White's name in years. For a while Babs had had her own
apartment in Milton, a little studio above the hardware store,

27

about twenty miles from Huntington, but when she lost her job as barmaid in the Village Bar & Restaurant she returned home to live with her mother, and it was during this time—sitting on the edge of her bed in the same room where she'd spent her childhood, the walls still plastered with the Huntington pennants and class pictures—that she discovered she was pregnant and told Connie the news. When it became obvious that Barbara wasn't going to reveal the name of the father, Connie called Dr. Amundsen, the town G.P., who reassured her by saying that at least she's not getting an abortion, "she's having the child isn't she? Isn't that enough?" as a way to indicate to Connie that possibly she underestimated her daughter and that taking on the responsibility of being a mother was potentially the best thing Babs could do. Though the doctor secretly believed that Barbara should get an abortion, he would never say anything like that to Connie LaRosa, whom he'd known for twenty-five years, first as a patient and most recently—or at least since his wife had died—as a close friend. And now that the baby was here what difference did it make? The baby—it, *she*—was white, so at least that cancelled out Henry Quire Jones, the school bus driver who lived in Marshfield, as a possible father. When Barbara was in the first stages of labor she called the doctor and he drove her in the middle of the night to the hospital in Concord and delivered the baby, whose last name, on the birth certificate issued by the Huntington Town Clerk, was the same as Barbara's. Both Connie and Dr. Amundsen assumed that Barbara knew who the father was, but neither had been successful in getting her to talk. Connie even went so far as to read her daughter's diary, something she'd been doing for years, but there wasn't even the slightest hint, as she later explained to the doctor. Barbara didn't care what anyone in the town thought; she'd been a kind of walking scandal sheet since her sophomore year in highschool, and almost enjoyed the feeling of knowing other people were talking about her, watching her, tittering to themselves as she walked by. It pointed out to her, without her consciously knowing it, the emptiness of their own lives, and though she was unhappy and even lonely at times, she never regretted anything and on the contrary felt a sense of achievement at having stepped beyond the ordinary limits of small town life.

At birth, Mary LaRosa weighed 9 pounds, 9 ounces.

Dr. Amundsen set his pipe in the ashtray when Barbara entered his office, a suite of small rooms on the ground floor of his house, not far from the center of town. During the time he'd practiced in Huntington he'd delivered almost the entire under twenty-five years of age population: Sally, Agnes, Bob and Barbara herself. His wife, who had grown up in nearby Marshfield, and whose desire to return to the scene of her childhood had been the reason they had settled here, had died ten years before; their only child, Susan, was presently living in California. He was alone; but where once it might have occurred to him to move elsewhere, a big or medium sized city perhaps, he never thought about it now. He enjoyed his life, even the sense of being alone, the company of his patients especially, and was amazed that he'd somehow progressed in time, from the avid medical student in the pinstriped suit that was too small for him and the wave of black hair that fell over his eyes whenever he bent forward, to the white haired, still diligent and alert but more often absentminded, nearsighted image that confronted him in the mirror each morning. In his office he wore wine-colored cardigans or vests; on home visits—which he only made locally—he worked in his shirt sleeves. There was no reason to be formal here, everyone knew him, treated him with deference, and even people who didn't know him well called him "Doctor."

If you're going to nurse your baby Intrauterine Devices (IUDs) are highly recommended by most doctors since it usually takes about three months after the baby's born to fit a diaphragm.

That was the information Barbara wanted.

"Since you're not ovulating it's highly unlikely that you'll get pregnant." Dr. Amundsen wondered whom Barbara was

29

sleeping with now—maybe a clue to Mary's father: he'd ask Connie the next time they spoke. He wished Barbara felt comfortable enough to confide in him. He was a good listener and encouraged the young women who visited him to unburden themselves of their problems, their fears of getting pregnant, for instance, and had learned not to flinch at the details of his young patients' pre-marital sexual experiences. While he interviewed and examined his patients he took notes and occasionally, with their permission, dictated into a tape recorder, information which he later transcribed into the patient's record. While his wife was alive she'd done most of the secretarial work, and even Susan, before she'd gone west, had done her best to help out; now most of the Doctor's evening hours were divided between editing the tapes of the voices of all the people who passed through his office, seeing Connie, and listening to The Redsox on the radio.

"I'm down to my normal weight at last, but still feel heavy around the stomach. The baby wakes up at 3 A.M. but since I've been feeding her solids I don't have that much milk. If I had some extra money I'd buy a new pair of jeans—none of my old clothes fit me anymore."

Dr. Amundsen didn't recommend birth control pills. If Bob hadn't missed that layup in the last minute Huntington would have come home state champions. The baby looked healthy: the doctor examined it, weighed it, gave *her* her first shot—and she fell asleep in Barbara's arms as she chatted with the doctor which was like taking a pill in itself. As in the expression "you're a pill" or "he's a good pill" meaning someone who gives comfort, encouragement, advice. Even the most expensive prophylactics (12 for 12 dollars) dull the sensation.

On the doctor's desk, between his appointment calendar and the large kidney shaped ashtray where he propped his pipe, there was a framed photo of his daughter Susan, whom he hadn't seen in over a year. As he talked with Barbara, or with any of the other girls who visited him, for that matter, it was hard not to imagine her, first: in bed with a man, an anonymous man since he'd never met any of her recent boy-friends, sleeping beside her. Secondly: in a doctor's office, much like his own. He could hear her voice:

"I think I'm pregnant." Or:

"I want to be fitted for a diaphragm."

He saw her superimposed on the girl sitting opposite him, the baby in Barbara's arms his granddaughter, named after his wife, not Barbara or Mary—these people were strangers: the doctor looked sad. Possibly Susan had a baby already and was embarrassed—ashamed!—to tell him. A baby without a father: but there was always that strange man, moaning in his sleep. The man he imagined lying beside her, whose face he couldn't see, and who was having what the doctor guessed was a bad dream. There was the secret baby in a crib in the corner, and the woman who was a combination of his daugh-ter and his wife crossed the room and prodded it with her index finger to see if it was still breathing. How could she not think he'd understand if she told him she was pregnant? Any man she brought home he'd embrace with open arms. All the reactions and interactions and recriminations of the past were over; he fixed himself a Jack Daniels on the rocks ("I can't sleep," Sally said, "the pills you gave me don't work") and turned on the tape.

"I LIKE LONG HAIR," BOB PRICE said, meaning *your* hair, Sally assumed. It was the summer before they were married, she'd just begun working at the diner, and had mentioned to someone sitting at the counter that she was thinking of getting her hair cut short; pixie-style, like Mia Farrow. Bob's interest in her physical appearance, that he noticed her at all, came as a shock, and the more attention he gave her, the more they worked together and brushed by one another in the narrow aisle behind the counter, the more she began to feel like a different person, more herself than any image she could summon up or imagine. Though she'd looked down on Bob all the time they'd been classmates in Huntington, she began to weigh and attempt to balance the things he said, realizing that during their school years they'd never spoken directly, one to one. And it was hard to ignore him; he was there when she showed up for work at nine in the morning; and when she left, at five o'clock, he was still there, along with his father, her boss at the time, "Old Man Price." Sally had never thought of Bob as a romantic person; the only thing that set him apart from the other boys in town, in her mind, was his height. "There's the tall one," she'd say to herself, it was a kind of instant recognition, but the two—when they passed on the street or in the hallway at school—never even said hello. Bob's friends were the other guys at school who were

33

interested in sports, the jocks, and his girlfriends—though Sally hardly kept track of such things—were the cheerleaders, girls half his size or so it seemed when you saw him with his arm around one of them, girls who were sophomores and freshmen when he was a senior and who were attracted to Bob for his reputation as local hero (just floating in the periphery of his attention was a kind of status symbol). Until she met Agnes Sally thought of herself in a world of her own, and knew enough about herself to realize she was better off not inflicting her feverish nun-like qualities on anyone else. It was Agnes who articulated her own negativity and hostility to people like Bob and small town life in general, and her friendship represented a small island of sanity—a place Sally could actually point towards—in the world outside. When Agnes said something Sally recognized in her words an accurate description of what she herself was feeling but had been frightened of admitting ("you're so timid," Agnes would say), and her first attempts at writing were prompted by the need to put into her own words the ideas and attitudes she'd learned from her friend.

The train doesn't stop in Huntington anymore. Why, I can remember the time when you could hear the whistle from five miles off and the kids, you kids, used to stop what you were doing and race off to the station as if the Pied Piper were calling your names, each individually: Come aboard, come aboard—and people would get off and on and wave goodbye, girls on their way to college would press their faces to the tinted glass while their parents and boyfriends and other friends who'd remained at home to take jobs as waitresses or gas station attendants wiped the tears of regret from their eyes as they waved goodbye. And old Hank Jones would hoist the luggage from his old dolly onto the rack above your seat and you'd ride out of town, triumphant, the noon whistle shrieking in your ears. Goodbye, Huntington. See you later. Au revoir!

When Agnes left town Sally tried to make friends with Sue

Amundsen, the doctor's daughter. Sally envied the younger girl, first for having a father—her own father had died the summer after highschool—but mainly for having a father who was practically the only person in town Sally could talk to, now that Agnes was gone, in any reasonable way. Consequently, she used her relationship with Susan as an excuse to visit the Amundsen household whenever she imagined the doctor was alone.

Susan was still in highschool. Cheerleading practice Tuesday and Friday. Bob was at the diner. The doctor looked up and turned off the tape.

"Sally dear," Agnes's letter began. The inversion of the two words made Sally pause, light a cigarette.

There were magazines sold on every city street corner, from outdoor newsstands to tobacco shops, in which famous basketball players posed with young blond girls whose first names were Roxanne, Roseanna, Babs, Mandy and Ilona. The athlete held a basketball in one hand, palming it, the fingertips of his other grazing the breasts of the girl nearest him. Jacob sat at his desk in his office, during lunch hour, turning the pages.

"When you get off the bus at Port Authority take a cab to our apartment."

Agnes's handwriting was legible and girlish and Sally was grateful for her tone: decisive, direct—no mention of Bob, no questions asked. As she reread the letter Sally remembered the afternoons they'd spent together, on the porch of Agnes's house or upstairs in Agnes's bedroom, bent over identical paperback editions of *Six Plays* by August Strindberg, making notes in the margin as they prepared for the school play.

"My mother was well-born, she came of quite humble people, and was brought up with all those new ideas of sex equality and women's rights and so on. She thought marriage was quite wrong. So when my father proposed to her, she said she would never become his *wife*. . . ."

Bob: "I think it would be good for you to get away" or

35

(laughing): "New York? You must be kidding!" Or: "Are you sure it's safe?" Or: "My father's coming for dinner tonight. Let's talk about it then."

Old man Price drank his coffee black. Blank.

The conductor walked through the car of the train shouting: "Huntington, Huntington."

Henry Quire Jones, Jr. sat down at the counter and ordered a milkshake. He watched Sally, as she turned her back to him, focusing on the knotted apron at the base of her spine.

"No, I've never been to New York, Mrs. Price. You thinkin' of goin'?"

Jan. 5. Went to see Susan today, but she wasn't home. The doctor asked if anything was wrong and I lied and said "no." He asked about Bob's leg, and I sort of shrugged as if it wasn't important. I think he must know something's wrong and is just waiting for me to open up. He looked surprised when I asked if I could get him anything, even though it's something I always ask. He never comes into the diner and I miss the chance to wait on him. He asked if I'd make a pot of tea and I told him I knew where everything was. We sat in the dining room and drank tea together. There was a white manila folder on the table but I'm not sure if it was "my" folder. When Susan came home (she was still wearing her cheerleading outfit) she looked annoyed—as if my presence there bothered her—so I left after a few minutes telling them I had to get back to the diner. I don't think Bob notices anything, but who knows?

THE NIGHT BEFORE TONY
arrived, he was their first house guest ever and consequently
his arrival necessitated a small conference, Jacob, in answer
to his wife's question: what is your brother like—(Jacob neg-
lected to tell Agnes that Tony was really his half-brother, his
mother's son by an earlier marriage) warned her that (as far
as he remembered, he hadn't seen Tony in almost five years)
he liked to sleep late, lie in bed and smoke cigarettes and read
the newspaper or whatever magazine was lying around
(Jacob didn't know why he was telling his wife these things:
Tony's laziness was hardly his most endearing characteristic
and Jacob knew that Agnes was tentative about meeting him,
and the upcoming visit). The morning after Tony's arrival,
Jacob had left for work, Agnes lay in bed, wondering what
she'd say to this stranger if they ever found themselves, as it
seemed they would if she decided to get out of bed and enter
the living room where he was sleeping, face to face across the
kitchen table.

Usually she went back to sleep for an hour or two after
Jacob departed. If he wanted, she'd get up and fix his breakfast, she insisted that she didn't mind since she wanted a
reason to get up, she felt lazy when she spent half the morning in bed, but even before they were married and living
together on the top floor of a brownstone in the South End of
Boston which they rented from one of Jacob's instructors at

37

Tufts, he insisted, in turn, that he needed the time, those few moments, alone in the morning ("to get my head straight") before going to work.

Bachelor habits. What was a wife for anyway? Even on weekend mornings when they would both sleep late and Agnes, in housecoat or nightgown, would make the breakfast while he read the papers, so leisurely they couldn't believe there was nothing urgent about their existence ("we're just like everyone else," Agnes would say to herself, as she laid out the strips of bacon on a paper towel and wiped the grease from the pan), Jacob would complain about the way she made his eggs, about the strength or weakness of the coffee, until finally—and all for the better as far as Agnes was

---

Beth Myles, the young wife of Frank Myles who managed the supermarket on the edge of town, and whom Frank had met a few years ago in Boston, had just left the doctor's office, not in the best of shape. After growing up in a big city she was having a hard time adjusting to small town life, didn't have any close friends ("Have you met Sally Price yet?" the doctor asked) and worst of all was trying without much success to have a baby. She'd stopped by the doctor's office ostensibly to get her valium perscription renewed and to find out the name of a gynecologist in Concord, but most of all she just wanted someone to talk to, though seeing the doctor always made Beth wish she'd waited awhile before getting married or that she'd chosen someone older; in comparison to the doctor her husband seemed like a big baby.

"Frank wants a family, a big family, at least he says so—and now he's begun to make me feel guilty whenever I don't feel like sleeping with him—he thinks the way to have a baby is to make love every night, and that if we do it every other night or only twice a week we'll miss the right time. Of course he doesn't know what he's talking about and when I try to explain to him that there are only a few days of every month when a baby can be conceived I know he's not even listening to me. And I also know it's stupid of me to keep taking valium when I want to get pregnant but on nights when we do make love I can never fall asleep. Frank seems to think that making love"—(and here the doctor almost wished she'd be less intimate, he was beginning to flash on his daughter again)—"is for his plea-

38

concerned—they exchanged roles: "You cook all week" "But *you* work"—a logic which allowed them to transcend the normally confused state of their domestic routine.

Before leaving, after he'd eaten breakfast, Jacob came in to the bedroom to say goodbye, as he usually did.

"Is Tony still sleeping?"

The window of the bedroom faced the park, where the day before yesterday, a woman—Agnes's age—had been attacked by a "band of youths" (that's what the newspaper had said) while bicycling in broad daylight.

"It happens everyday," in answer to Tony's question about whether the park was safe.

"Was she raped?"

---

sure and to make babies, he doesn't think—and I must admit every man I ever slept with before Frank was like that too—that I could possibly feel anything or experience anything, that I'm there for his use—and most of the time, let me tell you, I'm not feeling a thing, and I know Frank hates it when I just lie there. . . ."

Though he hated to admit it to himself, the doctor was glad to see her leave. He had a dinner date with Connie LaRosa—she was going to stop by at six—and he wanted to take a shower and change his clothes. Hearing the stories of people like Beth made the doctor feel helpless and apprehensive (what was the world coming to anyway?), and for about fifteen minutes after she left he sat at his desk with a copy of The Concord Monitor spread open before him mumbling to himself—too lazy and preoccupied to even light his pipe or fix a drink. It was the time of day when he felt most oppressed by his daughter's absence, especially when all he wanted to do—he'd seen his last patient—was relax. With his wife and daughter he could talk about anything that was on his mind, and it was necessary, a habitual necessity but a necessity nonetheless, to get whatever he was thinking off his chest. Talking about his feelings, discussing them with someone else, relieved him of the burden, and without this recourse the feelings and thoughts just built up, like a tower of small bricks which someone had labored over for years. During the past few months the doctor had caught himself talking outloud: in the mirror while he was shaving or when fixing himself dinner, or afterwards, washing the dishes. And now he had broken his favorite cup,

Agnes heard Tony yawn and imagined his naked body under the sheet she had given Jacob to take to his brother (arms and legs dangling over the edges of the couch, he was staring at the ceiling, smoking a cigarette). She stood at the window, watching a man in a gray sweatsuit jog down Central Park West in the rain. From three flights above the street she could see the windshields of the cabs lined up at the light at the corner of 79th Street. Then the light changed and the cars headed towards her, some faster, some lagging behind, like horses on a wet track. A young woman and her child, in identical yellow slickers, stood on the edge of the curb, waving for a cab. The presence of the park across the street made life in New York more tolerable for Agnes; when it rained

in anger, smashed it against the side of the sink. When he discovered himself talking aloud it was like coming out of a momentary trance, the dish would fall from his hand or he'd cut himself shaving. Sometimes he would carry on imaginary conversations with one of his patients—Sally Price, for instance—or with his wife, or daughter—and sometimes he realized that he was addressing Connie LaRosa. She was the one person in Huntington with whom he could talk openly, and who responded by giving him her undivided attention. At fifty-five (he was singing to himself in the shower) he was in good health, still thin, long white hair floating across his forehead like a badge of elegance, not old age. He wasn't a vain person, but the attention of his women patients made him aware of his physical appearance, since each day brought one or the other into his office and he couldn't not be aware of their physical presences at such close proximity. Twice a week he drove to the high-school gym and played basketball with Bob Price, Frank Myles, and the other young men about whom he'd heard so much, and who came to see him too, usually about minor physical ailments, as an excuse to talk to him about *their* problems, possibly as a ploy to find out for themselves how much their wives had discussed, how much he knew. Though he was almost thirty years older than most of them he had no trouble keeping up with the pace of the game for about a half hour. After that he was content to stand on the sidelines breathing heavily and compare the weary specimens dragging themselves up and down the court. He felt sorry for Bob Price, who was

40

there seemed to be some purpose, the nourishment of the trees and flowers. Growing up in the country she loved to walk in the rain, or stand outside in the summer and raise her arms and face towards the sky till she was soaked and her dress stuck to her breasts and legs and her mother, watching from the window of their house, called her inside, frightened that someone in a passing car (since she did have breasts, and she was wearing nothing under her dress) would see her, or one of the prissy, matronly spinsters who lived down the street would complain: complain to Agnes's mother, to the schoolboard or to the town selectmen: we can't have our young people exposing themselves on every street corner. . . . She was dancing to the rain, like an Indian;

out of shape, and whose clumsiness nullified his enormous height advantage, remembering when Bob was a senior in highschool and the momentary flash of excitement when it was mentioned in the local newspaper that scouts from colleges in the northeast were attending games right in town, just to see him. The doctor usually attended one game a year, taking Connie with him, but the team had gone downhill since Bob's day— in fact, something about the entire school, athletics and academics both, had disintegrated. The reading score for seniors was well below the state average, and only about five percent of the graduating class continued on to college. At a recent town meeting, the highschool principal, Margaret Kinnard, had told the doctor that many of the seniors, both male and female, were thinking of enlisting, figuring that if they didn't go to college they'd eventually be drafted anyway.

When the doctor went back over the events in his life he realized that he'd made one big mistake: he had spent too much time and energy trying to remain in control (the word appeared in bright italicized neon when he thought of it), in creating a wall or moat around himself which kept him apart from anything potentially dangerous or threatening. He had set goals for himself, and followed a plan, which in retrospect seemed very modest, always in the realm of what was possible. He'd always imagined himself a slightly heroic figure for having accomplished what he'd wanted to do, but in recent years the sense that on the surface his life was a carbon of countless other lives, admirable, useful, but unexception-

expressing a part of herself that she'd never thought about and which remained unblemished despite the exigencies of her new life in the city where just standing at her bedroom window, half-naked, made her wonder whether anyone was watching.

Over dinner the night before they'd discussed Tony's life in California, and now Agnes saw herself repeating the questions she'd asked yesterday ("what are your plans?") in an attempt to stimulate conversation with this man who was her brother-in-law ("they don't even look alike!") by definition but who might well have been a total stranger, someone whom Jacob had met on the street, or, if they lived in the

---

able in any way, emerged like a cloud on what he thought of as the beginning of his old age. In order to do something new or exciting one had to lose control, if only slightly, and allow the unexpected or random to take place. A sense of order resulted in accomplishment on a certain level, but what about the higher sense of order which made it possible to forget oneself and what one was doing; forget that one ever had any goals or plans. It was possible to keep one's goals in mind and still open a door to the possibility of chance. Years of living alone had made him self-critical. If he had been a heavy drinker he'd probably be the type who wept on the shoulders of strangers in roadside bars. ("Hey Pete, you better take the doctor home.") The man sitting beside him was drunk also—he was just passing through Huntington, and had a room at the Bare's Inn, the local motel on the outskirts of town.

"Did I scare you dear?"

It was Connie, a chiffon scarf knotted loosely at the open collar of her tan blouse (she was wearing a matching pair of slacks, and sandals with 1 inch heels), looking seductive, as she often did, and somehow out of place in the doctor's house.

"I knocked, figured you were taking a shower, the door was open—what's the matter? You don't mind that I came in?"

Again, he'd been thinking of something else, he'd been mouthing the words to "Ebb Tide"—remembering the way Giselle Mackensie or Snooky Lanson or Russell Arms or Dorothy Collins used to perform it on Your Hit Parade which he had watched with his wife in this very living room twenty-five years before. It was during the time

42

country, picked up hitchhiking and brought home for her to feed.

"They couldn't have been more than 12 or 13. . . . When I first saw them I thought: they're just kids—and didn't think twice. I mean, it's just not in my nature to be suspicious of everyone I see. Then two of them came up behind me, two in front. There was no one else around but I cried out anyway, what else could I do, thinking what they wanted was the bike—why would these kids care about me—when one of them clamped his hand over my mouth and the other started dragging me into the bushes. The last thing I remember was seeing my bike lying on the path where they'd stopped me,

---

before Susan was born and they had yet to make many close friends in the town. It was before Babs, Connie's daughter, had been born, before people like Elizabeth Myles or Sally Price came and told him their life stories. To all the women who complained to him and asked advice he wanted to say one thing: do something else, change your life. Move on. Leave this town. Get divorced, find a job. He wanted to tell them what they wanted to hear in the hope that the echo of their own thoughts in someone else's mouth would be enough to light the spark and set them all into motion. His own wife had had too much energy, suffered from high blood pressure, tended to be over excitable and easily angered—but at least, or so the doctor hoped, she was never bored. "Time to take your pill, dear." This house where they had lived together reverberated like a canyon—you shouted out your name, sang it aloud, and it came back to you, in an avalanche, buffeted by 50 mile an hour winds. Somehow all the detritis of the past fitted together: every object in the house was a thing in itself and also had reference to a memory—the memory surrounded the object with an aura that represented something negative or positive or both, and at times the doctor couldn't help walking through the rooms without wanting to burst into tears.

The doctor liked having another woman around. Connie knew that if she wanted, and had the inclination, there was a big empty space—the house, the person—for her to fill. When she was with him in the house she pretended it was her home, and without stepping beyond the sanctified border which she sensed still existed, tried to simulate a situation where she and the doctor may as well have

43

but I'm sure I could recognize at least one of them. . . ."

Agnes usually smoked her first cigarette after morning coffee, and here she was now, two hours into the day and she hadn't even gone to the bathroom! It was her home, wasn't it? She could hear the strange man moving around inside, and wondered what Jacob had told him about her. Tony hadn't even appeared at their wedding, for which he'd apologized last night, winking to Jacob as if to imply "If I'd known you'd married someone like this. . . ." It was a detail Agnes was supposed to have not seen, and as she thought about it she began to feel the need to harden herself, as if both these men were strangers working against her, plotting something she didn't know anything about. She wondered if

---

been people who had lived together for such a long time they could anticipate each other's moods, wants and needs, without speaking. At least she was able to do this. Most often when she saw the doctor he was in a mood like this one—preoccupied, distracted, not really there. So she went about her business, making drinks, and in general chattering away—about anything (she knew he liked to talk about her daughter Babs who was one of his patients) as she imagined the doctor's first wife must have done and it was her energy and self-confidence, surprising in a woman who had lived by herself for almost fifteen years, that had attracted the doctor. He took the gin and soda water from her extended hand without looking up at her and returned, from force of habit, to the large leather chair behind his desk.

"I'm not your patient, you know," Connie said, trying to draw his attention, "and just because you're sitting there it doesn't mean I have to sit"—and she pointed to the chair where a half hour before Elizabeth Myles had sat, pouring out her secrets. Instead she leaned back against one corner of the desk, and held her glass to her forehead.

"I know you've probably had a hard day—I didn't have the best day either—but that part's over now and you know what you always say about enjoying our time together. When I stood outside the door of this house tonight I said to myself: once I'm inside I'm going to forget everything that happened today, I'm not going to think about things that happened a long time ago, things I think about all the

Tony had been a close friend rather than a blood relation Jacob would have left him alone with his wife, so trusting. She knew that it was possible to transcend the erotic overtones of any situation by just acting naturally, as if "nothing mattered." What did she do normally? Jacob left for work, she went back to sleep or emerged from bed, went to the bathroom—naked, if she wanted, no one was watching—dressed, spent time getting dressed and thinking, if she wanted to, about what to wear, sat at the kitchen table (sometimes she didn't get dressed until after she'd had her coffee) trying to intertwine her morning thoughts with her last thoughts before falling asleep. Getting into bed at night usually prompted a rush of ambition, caught somewhere in the

time—why do you think I have trouble getting to sleep at night? Why do you think all these women come by at all hours of the day asking you to write them prescriptions for pills? They're lying awake and their husbands are out somewhere—I know that's true because I know what my own husband was like, and all you have to do is go down to Smiley's at any time and you'll find them all there: Frank and Bob and Pete—the whole gang. What do you think Sally Price does when her husband goes out at night—and she's an exception, she doesn't even have any kids! Bob Price would go crazy if she as much walked around the block without telling him. He goes crazy, anyway, or so I've heard, but you probably know about that better than I. Sometimes I think my thoughts and my memories and everything I know— and I'm talking about my instincts now, the little voices in my head which tell me what to do—are attacking me, and that part of me is locked behind some fortress warding off the attackers. I learned a long time ago that it's better to be doing something than to be thinking about doing something: when you're thinking all that's happening is that you're staring into space—and if anyone saw you in the actual act of thinking they'd think you were nuts. And sometimes I think that someone's watching me—when I lie in bed at night and can't sleep I remember that someone's watching everything I'm doing—and it makes me want to duck my head under the covers real quick."

The phone rang, the doctor placed his drink on the desktop, ran his hand through his damp hair, and lifted the receiver to his ear,

revolving door between the events of her waking life and her dreams. For the first year she and Jacob were married and especially in the months after they first came to New York Agnes would conscientiously check *Variety* and *Show Business* for auditions, and with Jacob's encouragement she'd spend an afternoon a week, sometimes more, in the wings of a deserted playhouse downtown, waiting her turn. A string of disappointments led her to believe that Jacob's encourage-ment hadn't been totally sincere, at least it was easiest to cast the shadow of blame on him, that he'd never really wanted her to be an actress and preferred her at home, even if it meant she was "doing nothing." The move from the West

---

said "Hello," then waited, and then again, "Hello, hello."

He was standing in front of the ocean in San Diego where he'd gone on his honeymoon, hand in hand with his wife as the waves rippled around their feet and ankles, the waves came from so far away and grew smaller when they touched the shore and the water was so warm it was possible to just dive under without thinking and you had to walk out, for miles it seemed, until the water was over your head, it was dawn and the beach was empty and the sound of the waves filled his head as he held the phone like a conch shell to his ear—and for all he knew he might just as well be listening to the heartbeat of anyone of the thousands of patients he'd administered to over the years: hovering over them with his stethoscope—staring distractedly into space as he listened. He had a manner of his own, didn't he—that's why they all came back, all these women—and their husbands too—(didn't Frank Myles come in just a week ago to ask if there was anything wrong with his wife? as if he knew she was telling the doctor everything, revealing herself completely)— "you can get dressed now Mrs. Price." She had beautiful shoulders. He and Con-nie: he wondered if the people in Huntington thought of them as "a couple." And they were a couple: it had crossed his mind more than once, now that Susan was gone, that they just get married—she could move in any time, sell her house, Babs and the baby could come too. It wasn't the furthest thought from his mind, at any rate. And maybe Susan would fly in from California for the wedding, just a simple service possibly not even in the church but with the Justice of the Peace ("we can have it right here") in front of the fireplace in the

Village, where they first lived, to Central Park West, had confirmed her belief that he wanted her as far as possible from a world which might threaten their marriage. If that's what being an actress meant, a threat. The level on which this was true was more vague, however, than the reality which Agnes could only partially accept about her acting ability, or lack of it. Was she really that bad? It was almost a relief not to want to be something. Jacob's pretensions about being a writer forced Agnes into the position of the person who lends encouragement, and she was good at it, even though she was only acting.

In a scene she imagined herself "being raped" (more apt

---

living room. There was a humming sound at the other end as if whoever had called were sending him a secret message—there was no melody or pattern i.e. no variations on a theme—nothing he could identify: Liszt, Chopin, Grieg. He loved them all, he wanted to be loved—and his patients responded, in this sense he was just like them. Maybe Julius LaRosa—Connie's cousin—would come and sing "Ebb Tide" at their wedding!

A fly was buzzing in the room and Connie, using a section from the newspaper, swatted it, losing her balance. The charm bracelets she wore on each wrist caught the late afternoon light and the doctor saw something flicker, like headlights in a storm—the body, hers, his wife's, his wife to be, was moving towards him, a blur, weaving and bobbing like a boxer. He'd heard there might be a storm that night, Bob Price had mentioned it at the diner this morning and maybe he'd been so sequestered in his office listening to the stories of other people's lives he hadn't noticed his own was just passing by, not sadly, but like a series of lights on the bottom of a bridge which you watch from a train window—you're coming into a town with your wife and all your possessions: moving for the first and last time, signing your name on the dotted line, lifting the furniture up the steps where a few weeds were growing in the cracks, carrying your wife over the threshold—"This is our home now, my darling." The phonecall was forgotten. He didn't even replace the receiver on the cradle. As Connie knelt beside his chair, encircling his legs with her arms, he knew he didn't want anyone else to call. Not Sally Price or Beth Myles, or anyone. His day was over.

47

for a movie than a play). Her assailants were black. She threw herself onto the bed, pushing upwards with her hands, tossing her head from side to side. She kicked, clamped her knees together, opened her mouth as if to cry out. The bed was a bed of grass, or gravel. "Thank you, Miss North. We'll be in touch." But when she emerged from the bedroom, a few minutes later, still in her nightgown, Tony was gone.

THE DINER WAS EMPTY. ON A small transistor radio hidden behind the display for disposable cigarette lighters, haircombs, flints, and a framed photograph of Bob in his basketball uniform (holding a trophy which partially obliterated the number 11 on his jersey), an anonymous orchestra played an uptempo arrangement of "Yesterday" to the porcelain counter, rotating stools, the trays of knives, forks and spoons, and the booths, encased in blotchy red upholstery, which lined the walls. When Bob was a kid, still in gradeschool, and his parents had first bought the diner, he would sit in one of the booths near the window, waving to everyone who passed, waiting while his father and mother scoured and cleaned the counters and mopped the floor so the place would look fresh when they reopened the next day. Years later, when he was in highschool, and the novelty of being able to think of the diner as his own had worn off, Bob would come in with his friends after basketball practice and crowd into the same booth near the street, reupholstered more than once since those early days, and comment obscenely (but under his breath, so his father wouldn't hear) whenever one of the girls or young women of Huntington passed by. By then his mother had died; Millie, who now worked in the kitchen, part-time, and who had taught Bob whatever he knew about being a short-order cook, was the head waitress. It had been Bob's idea, when still at school, and it was evident that he'd take over the business from his father, to convert the storage room in back into a playroom where the kids of Huntington could go in the afternoon. Pinball machines were shipped from Manchester; a pool table from Boston. Bob and his friends painted the room an odd shade of purple, which Millie said made her feel like throwing up, and decorated the walls with larger than life posters of Presley, James Dean, Marlon Brando in the black leather motorcycle jacket and cap he wore in *The Wild One* and The Grateful Dead. Despite Millie's lack of enthusiasm, the playroom flourished. There was no organized recreational center or community hall outside the school, and most of the parents of Bob's friends felt a mixture of resignation and relief that they at last had some idea where their sons and daughters went after class. The final addition to the playroom, a jukebox, made its appearance shortly after Bob's father retired. It had been Sally's idea, soon after she and Bob were married, but she gave her husband the credit. As long as the volume was kept at a moderate level and didn't disturb the customers in the diner itself there was no argument against having it, though those like Millie and Bob's father, who would like to have seen things remain as they were, looked askance when the idea was presented to them. (Neither Sally nor Agnes had ever spent much time in the diner. Rehearsals for the school play often lasted past the time the diner stayed open, and on other afternoons Sally either went directly home, to Agnes's house, or to the library. The other girls in their class thought of them as "snobs," but they didn't care.) In the center of the diner, a combination newspaper and magazine rack gave the area a sense of symmetry: it was a place to stop, linger at, on your way out or while waiting for coffee to go. Copies of The Concord Monitor, The Boston Herald-Examiner, The Globe, The Huntington Eagle (the local weekly paper), along with copies of Time, Newsweek, Good Housekeeping, The Enquirer, Cosmopolitan, TV Guide, Modern Screen, Outdoor Life, People etc. It was nine o'clock. As Sally entered she

50

heard the radio, turned on full blast, and still half-dazed from the sleeping pill she'd taken the night before thought that the music was coming from the jukebox in the playroom. "Bob?" There was no doubt in her mind that she was in the right place, though she was thinking of Agnes, and the letter she was intending to write, but the music and the stale atmosphere, reeking of ammonia and the solitude and sadness of people with no imagination but to clutter their surroundings with objects of interest only to the curious opener of a time capsule in some far-off century, filled her with a feeling of angst so familiar that by the time she'd deposited her pocketbook behind the counter she'd burst into tears.

She could stand there behind the counter, with her head against the cool imitation marble, and all the people in the town would wander past her and around her and Bob would enter as in a play from the doorway leading to the kitchen (he'd been in the bathroom all this time) and no one would notice, no one would see the look in her eyes or understand what it meant, or even ask her: Is anything wrong? You look tired, honey, didn't you sleep well last night? You could use a cup of coffee yourself. Not even Bob would dare to notice, since if he did he'd have to say something which meant, in turn, that Sally would have to respond. And at this point there was nothing either of them could say. The only difference between the conversations they had together and the casual banter they shared with their customers was that they gave each other permission to show anger or bitterness, even though such shows of emotion had recently been made superfluous by the slamming of a door or by turning over in bed and pretending one was asleep or by long periods of withdrawn silence, as if she had a mask or net over her head and could pass in and around her husband, as he could around her, pass within each other's orbit and never make contact, never touch. The only person she could talk to in this town was Doctor Amundsen, and the only chance she had to see him was on weekday nights when Bob left the house after dinner, left her alone to do as she pleased as long as she didn't do anything since Sally had never tested him by being out when he came home though she'd thought of it and even felt diffident about visiting the doctor whom she'd had a crush on since highschool and who was older than her father would have been if he were still alive but attractive, not in some fatherly way, but as an actor ages and still remains as young as the first famous characters he portrayed, an ageless wonder. "Where were you?" she could imagine Bob saying. For a change, it was she who'd gone out, and now he was sitting in the living room with the lights off, waiting for her. Sitting and smoking, he was already drunk, and Sally knew there was going to be trouble, a scene: skillets and plates flying through the air, black eye the next morning—she was due at the diner at nine, how would either of them get there on time? The customers who came in would be too tactful to ask questions, but in the same way everyone knew all the names of all the boys Barbara LaRosa was sleeping with so they'd know that The Prices, Bob and Sally, were having a fight ("Tsk, tsk.")

Stage directions, cast of characters: who would play Bob? The evening breeze caressed the trees. Sally dried her eyes and turned off the radio. In the end, he'd beg her not to go. He hated Agnes; he'd probably call her the first night she was gone. And when a few days passed and she still hadn't come back, as she didn't intend to do, he'd call again, threaten to come and get her if she didn't return on the next bus. Sally could make up the words and hear Bob recite them as he acted out the scene. "Sorry, but I think you're a little too tall for the part."

A WAY OF GREETING, A NOD, A handshake. "Glad to meet you," or "haven't we met before?" (Don't I know you from somewhere?) A way of saying "thank you" or "please" apologetically. (Some people say "I'm sorry" before they do something that would necessitate an apology afterwards.) Doormen who go out of the way to be polite, while secretly hating you, waiters and waitresses who know what you want before you say anything, who call you "Mr" or "Sir" when what you feel like is a little kid who's just tossed a stone through the plate- glass window of a store selling television sets and radios and household appliances you could never afford. The type of restaurant where someone meets you at the door and shows you to a table; a place where you have to call ahead for reservations, where the waitresses all wear long pleated dresses or low cut blouses and short skirts or just leotards and the waiters pull back your chair and help your girlfriend or wife off with her coat while you stand to one side wondering is he doing this to impress me, or her: what is he thinking? And it was possible that either the waiter or waitress, like the doorman, was just doing his or her job: that the outward show of courtesy was what made them successful at what was perhaps only a part-time stopgap profession, a way of earning a living before luck turned the corner and they were given a part which would take advantage of their innate abilities, dormant for so long.

Jacob took a deep breath as the elevator packed with office workers descended rapidly from floor to floor. He'd been working in the same building, at the same company, for over a year, long enough to become a fixture i.e. someone who was recognized, acknowledged, nodded to when he walked through the hallways or stepped in and out of the elevator, though no one except the people he worked with directly knew his name. People in elevators, like people crowded together on the subway at rush hour, rarely speak. There were a limited number of things to do to defy the intimacy of such a situation: watch the arrow above the door as it revolved counter clockwise to the number of the floor—in this case the lobby, denoted by the number 1—which was your destination, fold your newspaper into a narrow strip and lean it lightly on the back or shoulder of the person in front of you and read whatever article or headline was visible, think about something else as a way of distracting yourself from the feeling of self-consciousness at being so close to other people—it was almost like dancing with someone you didn't know, but whom you'd seen approaching across the dancefloor wondering if he was coming towards you, to pick you out—and now you're in his arms, not talking or thinking, but with your head resting on the collar of his shirt or the lapel of his jacket, his hand guiding you towards him as the music evolves like a circle in time to a melody you know by heart.

Jacob spent most of his time at work, when he wasn't actually working, and during his lunch hour, making mental and written notes: describing people, what they wore, the things they said, facial gestures, intonations, special personality characteristics or physical distortions. Sometimes he had trouble naming things, like what was the name of the fabric of the blouse of that girl who had recently begun working in the office adjacent to his (he made another note to ask Agnes about this), and on warm days he'd pick a street corner and lean back against a car and try to describe the building he was facing as best he could, as well as everything else that was happening—the people passing by, a detail, an aberration, what it felt like to be alive at that moment. His job, working in the reference department of a publishing company, involved indexing a huge updated book of quotations modelled after Bartletts Familiar Quotations but including work from more contemporary writers, and it was easy—as he sat at his desk—to let his thoughts drone on beyond the point where there was any "you" or "I" or person of substance to be found, easy—as he observed from the people around him for whom this job was their life's work, their career (because he liked so many of his co-workers he was careful not to feel overly supercilious)—to lose the sense that there was anything more important than what he was doing. To make it seem important the context (that it was just a job for which he was receiving payment) had to be erased; the least one could do was pretend that one was working out of sheer pleasure, or love. Jacob invariably completed his work in a few hours, so rather than having a long period of time when it would look to his boss that he wasn't doing anything he spread out the work over the course of the day, leaving a little for the last minute, while relaxing for long stretches in between. It was possible to pretend to be attentive to what he was doing (he'd had a lot of practice, as a student in college, feigning interest in his work) while his attention was directed on something else, a train of thought, a fantasy, the right word to fill in the blank in the description of the girl across the room who just started work a week ago and whose name Jacob didn't even know (he was surprised that no one had introduced them) since he didn't feel free, as a married person (and what difference did that make?) to leave his office which was in effect one of a number of cubicles set into the center of a larger open area, this wasn't a dance floor after all and he just couldn't approach as if she were an object like a rock or piece of driftwood that happened to wash up on the shore as he was strolling by, he needed a reason that was both innocuous and somehow served the purpose of making their initial encounter seem meaningful (since later, if there was a later,

55

and they found themselves in bed together, the blouse whose fabric he couldn't identify tossed carelessly over the arm of a chair, it would be possible to reconstruct their initial thoughts and impressions of one another, as well as the encounter itself, without embarrassment).

She was in the elevator, a step away from him, and he could see the top of her head, her hair (easy to describe in terms of color and smell but was it the type of hair that she put up in pin curlers every night? did women still do such things?) held in place by a single amber barrette that interrupted the flow of the strands just below her neck, he could see her profile, her nose small and straight, and her lips with a little ridge of flesh in the center which meant she could probably look arrogant or scornful or tough if she wanted (she could certainly take care of herself!), and mean it, the expression was an invitation that allowed you to think "everything is possible" at the same time realizing the possibility of disappointment was so great it was perhaps better to watch someone else make the attempt, to keep your distance until something greater and more elusive than your own simple desires or sense of curiosity drew you together.

There was always the temptation, since they usually shared the elevator together at noon, to follow her when she left the building and in that way find out more about her, but the impulse to do this still seemed a little extreme, and reminded him of something he'd done as a child, playing "sleuth"—which meant picking a person at random on the street and then following him or her home—with his childhood friends. He knew that if he did that it would be placing the object of his attention out of the realm of possibility, make it too much like a game or part of a fantasy. If they ever did meet he would perhaps have to tell her that he'd spent his lunch hours following her from restaurant to store or wherever, and the thought itself, just the idea, made him wonder if for his own protection he'd better pursue the fantasy, at least once, and by so doing make certain nothing real could ever happen. The question his instinct presented him with formed the center of a small problem that was actually very tidy. He didn't know if he wanted something to happen with anyone, and if he did how could he make that happen given his present circumstances. How to deal with the potential consequences was also a mystery to him. Until the new girl had come to the office there hadn't been any reason, none strong enough, to move him from point A (his life with Agnes) to any other place (and now the whole subject was beginning to tire him).

At the corner of 14th Street and 3rd Avenue he bought the New York Post. The man at the newsstand, face partially obscured behind the bearded folds of a scarf, said "thank you," as Jacob placed the correct change on the small tray and took his place on the curb among the crowd of office workers, secretaries, mail clerks, and executives of various rank (but how could you tell who was who?) waiting for the light.

If he insisted, Agnes would prepare a lunch for him to take to work. She could do it the night before so she wouldn't have to get up ("but I don't mind!") so early. He could buy The Times in the morning, he hated The Post anyway, and read it over a sandwich or possibly even a plum or an apple, depending on the season, in the privacy of his office.

The sight of the girl behind the counter at The Central Lunch, a restaurant between 13th and 14th Streets on Broadway, reminded Jacob of Sally, who was coming to stay with them next week.

When I get up—she would sleep on the couch, as Tony had done— I'll be careful not to wake her.

In highschool his mother prepared lunch for him, but before reaching school he'd throw the brown paper bag containing the sandwich and the piece of fruit into the trash, preferring the lunch from the school cafeteria which his friends ate and which he payed for out of his allowance (this meant that often, lacking the money, he didn't eat anything except a chocolate bar or a container of milk). When anyone asked him why he was so thin he said that it was due to all the years of eating only one big meal a day, but he never told his parents that he wasted all those lunches, felt guilty now that his mother was no longer alive and he could picture her fixing his sandwich each morning before she went to work, standing in the narrow kitchen: lunch for himself, his father, and for Tony when he lived at home. ("I just never liked other people watching me eat," he confided to Agnes one night, "it made me self-conscious, everyone taking their sandwiches out of bags or spooning up the awful stuff they served in the cafeteria, everyone comparing the food their mothers had made for them and then complaining about it afterwards and how horrible they felt—I just decided to exempt myself from it all and after awhile my body somehow adjusted and I didn't feel hungry, though I didn't have a big breakfast I did manage to eat a lot at dinner and I think I had a snack, milk and cookies, when I got home from school and no one would be home and I could sit and eat as I pleased, listening to the radio, with no one watching me.")

It's possible to be smarter than everyone else without revealing it or lording it over other people in an attempt to make them feel inferior. But intelligence, like the single marbles of an abacus a baby plays with on the side of his or her crib, reveals its true nature by passing from mere practical usefulness into a form of compassion which is the first sign of wisdom. Until all the facts, like reprimands from a strict parent, dissolve in mid-air, gyrating in a sullen performance, like fists pounding an imaginary assailant's chest out of self-defense, till the only words that can be discerned are "see you later" or "I'm lost."

"Jacob. . . . I'd like you to meet Denise. She just started working here."

The girls in the diner wore their names on their collars. But did that mean, if you frequented the same restaurant everyday, you could grow so familiar with the people who worked there that you might address them by their first names, without being introduced formally?

When he returned from work Agnes never said "Did you have a good day?" She was always home when he arrived.

Reward for absence was a dinner, not at a restaurant, where the waitresses could be admired secretly, but at a kitchen table where the faded petals of tulips and geraniums, Agnes's favorite flowers, fell from a vase onto the checkered cloth.

"Would you like a light?" It was he, Jacob, offering Agnes a match, cupping his hands around the flame. Smoking a cigarette was a good way of postponing the question of whether or not the person you were with would come home with you that night. They had just met, and were standing in the windy streets outside Symphony Hall, and as she tipped her head forward her fingers steadied his hand around the flame (sometimes it wasn't even necessary to ask the question).

The clock above the counter in the crowded restaurant—he was sitting at the counter—informed him that there was still time for a cup of coffee before returning to work. "Betty" he wanted to cry out, as the waitress spun around, but her smile (like Fra Pandolf's in Browning's poem "My Last Duchess") was for the customer behind him, waiting his turn.

THE "OLD BUILDING," MEANING
the "old highschool," where Bob and Sally's parents and
where Agnes's father (her mother, whose own parents had
been French, attended a lycée in Switzerland) had gone to
school and about which, when they were alive, they would
reminisce endlessly, was still standing—a quarter mile off
Route 7, down Flanders Road. Bob remembered driving out
to the school with his father, and sitting in the car while Mr.
Price told him the story about how he'd first met Bob's
mother (this was after Bob's mother had passed away, and
coincided with the start of Bob's own highschool career).

"We used to sit under that tree and watch the leaves
change, pretendin' to study—not only us but the other kids
too, all of us, till it turned dark." He pointed out the car
window at a tree which had no special significance to Bob,
except as an object outside himself he might attempt to mas-
ter—in this case climb, notch by notch, till he reached the
highest branch. The memories that returned in the shape of
an oncoming thunderstorm budding on the horizon, a twist-
er—depending upon what part of the country you came
from—were absorbed by the halo of smoke rising from Mr.
Price's pipe as he absentmindedly slapped his son's knee,
shaking his head in disbelief.

"Then they came along and built that new building. . . ."

Bob had heard all this before. Sally had heard it from her

own father. The building of the new school had been a source of controversy and conversation and muted anger for years before the board of selectmen finally agreed to put the necessary funds aside, while making provisions to convert the old building into a community center ("there's no place for the kids to hang out except the back of that diner, right?"), despite its less than central location.

("Sally's thinking of taking a little trip to New York and we thought of asking your advice. . . .")

After his marriage, Bob began to realize, without articulating it to himself in any truly coherent way, how much of his interior world he'd inherited from his father. Despite his height, he remained his father's shadow, as inert as the shadow of a statue in the garden where the sun came out from behind the clouds for an hour each day, then disappeared. It was the garden of his own house, surrounded by a white picket fence that needed paint, where he'd hunted toads and snakes and lizards as a child. It was the darkness of the basement which he was forbidden to enter but where he went regardless to sit on an old board, reading by the dull glow of a flashlight whose batteries were dying, the out of date magazines Mr. Price brought home from the diner and which he stored in huge barrels the way some people keep old wine. That wine filled Bob's head, leaving a stronger impression than the words of his parents and teachers, more than the vague declensions in which Julius Caesar's heroics became nothing more than the words in a foreign language he could copy from the girl, one of those smart-asses, who sat across from him in Latin. Agnes North. It was she (and later Babs LaRosa) whose face appeared as he turned the pages of Police Gazette and Manhunter Magazine. A blindfolded girl whose red dress had been torn to reveal the tops of breasts and shoulders, blindfolded because Bob had kidnapped her and taken her to this very basement where twice a day he brought her food and water, but wouldn't give any of it to her unless. . . .

The "new building" housed not only the students of Huntington, but kids from the surrounding towns, Hopkinton and Bradford and Weare, went there as well. Henry Quire Jones, formerly chief porter on the train that once stopped in Huntington, was reincarnated as chief bus driver, head of a fleet of 5 yellow buses, one of which he drove each morning and again each afternoon from Huntington to the depot in Concord, a job which commanded only a fraction of the respect (though more salary) he'd received from the men and women of his own generation whose luggage he handled in the manner of an antiquarian, where for the students he drove to and from school he was the potential butt of a thousand jokes.

The "new building" resembled a factory. A modern factory, surrounded by baseball diamonds and asphalt basketball courts. "What's the old man complainin' about?" Bob asked himself as he walked down the spacious corridors for the first time. Because of his height he sat in the last row for all his classes, a secret bonus as it made cheating easier.

"Bob, I realize you're devoting most of your time after school to basketball . . . but there are other things that are important too."

In the bark of a tree back of the house where his father had put up his own private basketball hoop, Bob carved the initials A.N. & B.P. as a testimony to feelings he didn't even know he had.

"Sorry, but I have a date tonight."

"What about next week?"

"Why don't you call me then."

And when next week came:

"Oh, Agnes isn't home now. Who should I say called?"

He thought that if he burned a scar in his palm with the tip of a lit cigarette and word got around that he'd done it because she'd rejected him—well then maybe she'd realize that he was serious. Even his coach noticed that something was wrong and advised him to take the day off, get some sleep. A big game was coming up and there'd be scouts in the stands watching him. He walked alone down the empty streets through the autumn dusk, wondering whether he should call Agnes again one last time, even if it meant talking to her mother (he could always hang up when he heard her voice!) when the sound of a girl's voice from the enclosed porch of a nearby house broke the spell. Babs called his name, walked down the front steps of the house, reeling slightly as if she'd been drinking, and greeted him with a wave of a hand which sent the bracelets spiralling up her wrists and arms. In her white sweater, short white skirt and white ankle high boots, she looked as if she'd just returned home from cheerleading practice (while the truth was she'd been kicked off the squad for being a bad influence on the younger girls). Bob felt too numb to carry on any kind of normal conversation but after a few minutes found that it wasn't necessary to say anything.

"My mom's not home. Would you like to come in?"

The wall above her bed was covered with pennants and photographs clipped from movie magazines. The house was a mess. Didn't these people believe in cleaning up? And the bed was too short for him, too small for both of them. The springs creaked. If her mother came home . . . but Babs assured him, slipping her hand down the front of his pants, that that wouldn't happen. He turned over on his side till his bare back touched the wall and made a space for her beneath the sheets. She didn't remove her bracelets, and once when they exchanged places, she on top of him, the point of a miniature gold star scratched his cheek, drawing blood which she licked away.

"You mean you didn't use anything?"

"I never do."

"How do you know you're not going to get pregnant?"

He wondered what he would say when they saw each other the next day in school; and possibly it was the relief that she, unlike all the other girls, didn't expect him to say anything, that gave him the impetus to return to her house a few days later. And there she was, sitting on the swing on the enclosed porch, smoking a cigarette—"my mother won't be back till late"—as if she were waiting for him. Following her up the steps to her room, he knew that possibly if he came here again, and then again, he would be cured of his feelings for Agnes. And once, by mistake, as she lifted her arms and slipped her cashmere sweater over her head and knelt beside him, he called her Agnes, closing his eyes as he repeated the name, but to his surprise—and horror—she didn't seem to care.

THE MAIN ADVANTAGE OF SMALL-town life is the lack of heavy traffic (this is true also of Venice), automobile traffic, since the congestion caused by a plethora of gondolas and vaporetti mingling in the greenish waters wasting away the stones of the St. Marco gives one, more often than not, a reason to rejoice, a feeling of pleasure. There are other advantages as well: first, you're practically on a first-name basis with all your neighbors, you know everyone and everyone's children and the life stories of relatives you've never even met but heard about and seen in both wallet size snapshots and enclosed in cheap frames on living room end tables, larger than life. A small town is like a commune, at least on the surface, despite the sense one feels that once inside separate houses the members of each particular family go their separate ways, even if it's only a matter of movement from room to room: kitchen to bedroom to television etc. The negative side of this advantage is the lack of privacy which comes from being part of the non-stop comings and goings of your neighbors. There's the sordid underside of every act which causes raised eyebrows, even among the most progressive or liberal minded in any community. If you're still young, and go to sleep early, you might tiptoe downstairs in the middle of the night and hear your parents discussing the family down the street ("bootlegging? you mean they still do that?" "no, it's what he used to do—in

Texas—how do you think he made all his money, how do you think they live?"), you might wake to the sound of a door slamming and rush downstairs to find your mother smashing her best dishes, one by one, against the kitchen wall. Across the driveway that separates your house from your neighbor's you can see your sister's best friend undressing in the moonlight at her open window. (Perhaps she even knows you're watching her!) It's a world in which gossip follows the weather as the subject, or the actual content, of everyone's conversations. It's as if the decision to share the same geographical location, however arbitrary, gives you the privilege to create a sense of intrigue and drama by simply embellishing ordinary day to day events. This includes not only being able to imagine what your neighbors are like in bed, but knowing what they're like through first-hand experience.

WHEN THEY MOVED TO NEW
York from Boston, and before they'd found their own apartment, Agnes and Jacob stayed with Jacob's father in the
Bronx, in the same apartment where Jacob had spent the
first seventeen years of his life. Every morning he would
wake early and relive a brief episode from his childhood by
going out and getting the newspaper at the candystore on the
corner, then returning with it to sit at the kitchen table over
morning coffee. "Getting the newspaper" had been a Satur-
day and Sunday morning ritual, one of his first childhood
responsibilities. Now while Agnes, his wife, and his father
were sleeping, he mulled over the ads for apartments in the
back of The Times. Jacob's father, a retired vacuum cleaner
repairman and salesman, who had once owned his own store
and had somehow retired on his savings, fell asleep most
afternoons in front of the television in the living room. On
days when they weren't answering the few interesting ads
("interesting" meaning in this case apartments they could
afford) either by phoning the number listed in the ad or
actually journeying downtown to see the apartment, Jacob
took Agnes on a tour of his old neighborhood, pointing out
the building where he'd gone to public school and the
schoolyard where he used to play softball (odd how the walk
from his apartment to the school seemed so short, now, and
how the schoolyard—the center of a universe once—was just a

long stretch of broken concrete surrounded by wire fences), the delicatessen where he used to go to buy food on evenings when his mother was working—he and his father and Tony would make sandwiches for themselves, the apartment where his grandmother used to live and where Jacob had eaten lunch, every day, when both his parents were working. At night, on the foldout couch in the living room, he and Agnes "practiced perversions," or so they called it, too self-conscious to make love in the usual sense with Jacob's father

---

Some women who travel alone remove their wedding bands, in an attempt not to discourage complete strangers from starting conversations. They make up intelligent reasons for travelling from place to place, but what they're most interested in is who they might meet in the course of the trip. Sally had never travelled by herself before, and though it was an adventure to finally be out in the world and alone, she still wished there was someone with her—not so much to protect her as she'd felt on that first honeymoon visit to New York with Bob, but someone she knew well and with whom she could share her impressions. If a stranger asked her where she was from she'd tell him or her— there was no reason to lie—but beyond that she wondered what information she would divulge about herself if called upon. (Some women who travel alone lie about their name and where they come from as a means of protecting themselves, since meeting people on the road—and even sleeping with them, which is always possible—requires that at least one of the parties is a good judge of character: quick to get a take on just what this person sitting next to you is really like before you hop into bed with him . . . should we use our real names?) In Huntington it was a rare event when someone she didn't know entered the diner. She knew most of the people in town by their first names, everyone knew her. They all knew too much about each other, and the predictability of all their lives cancelled out any feelings of intimacy that might normally occur. Sally's main experience of the world outside Huntington was through the books she'd read, and her own imagination which lead her to assume every person in the world represented a different way of acting or responding—individual qualities overrode whatever common attributes might be possible, anyone could say anything, do anything, and she wouldn't be surprised. When she

so nearby. Being around someone like Jacob's father who had worked all his life and was now content "just to do nothing," plus the fact that Jacob genuinely enjoyed being back in the Bronx, in "the old neighborhood," made them lazy, and even their idea of perversion was a way of admitting to themselves that they were too tired to give or take real pleasure. It was only when their money started to run low and they found themselves on the verge of spending the money they'd planned to use for the apartment, the first

---

packed her suitcase and was dressing for the trip she wasn't thinking about who she might meet that day—or who would see her. She hadn't been planning on making an impression on anyone. She'd been thinking, despite herself, of Bob (who had left the house before her that morning, angry because she'd refused to sleep with him the night before) and the idea that this might be the last night in the house they'd lived in together for five years. She wouldn't miss any of it. She had a thousand dollars and hopefully she could find some kind of work in New York, possibly through Agnes's husband whom she knew worked for a publishing company. She would find a place to live—even if it was only a rented, furnished room—and go back to school at night. Her thoughts took her out of the present and cut her off from what she was looking at out the tinted windows of the half-empty bus which was overheated (it was spring, after all) and made her want to nod off and it wasn't until she reached Boston and was told that she had to change for the New York bus (there was a half-hour wait) that the finality of what she'd done took over. Goodbye Huntington. It didn't exist. If someone asked her where she came from, some stranger, she would tell them the truth—what difference could it possibly make?

"I've only had one lover—I've never done this before—"

But she couldn't tell that to anyone. Agnes knew, and the doctor. Her wedding ring slipped off easily and she dropped it in the bottom of her shoulder bag. She'd become hardened, inured, like all the other girls who came from small country towns to the big city. People would take advantage of her and she wouldn't even know what was happening until one morning she woke up in a strange apartment and the thousand dollars in her wallet was gone and she didn't even have a clean dress or a brush to comb her hair. By then even Bob

71

month's rent and security, that they began to see the necessity of making some move, and quickly, remembering all the plans they'd made in Boston just a few weeks before. The apartments listed in The Times were too expensive. The only way to find an apartment was to go to the neighborhood where they wanted to live and locate a real estate agency, even though that meant paying another sum of money to the realtor, usually a month's rent or in some cases a percentage of the yearly rent. The first apartment they saw by this

---

wouldn't want her back (he doesn't even want me now), and if Agnes or Jacob saw her on the street they'd look the other way. "I'm busy today, Sally, sorry—" There would be no alternative except to take an elevator to the 100th floor of one of those buildings where every window is a sheet of glass and propel herself like a human missile to the street below. "Class valedictorian, waitress in Price's Diner for five years."

It was 9:30 A.M. and the terminal was filling up. Young men in cowboy boots leaned back against the walls smoking cigarettes and occasionally spitting into soiled handkerchiefs, looking as if they'd slept in their clothing—if they'd slept at all. The terminal itself was a long narrow rectangle, with ticket windows on one wall and rows of plastic seats running in columns down the center, small TVs attached to each seat. At one end there was a glass door where you went when your bus arrived. Sally took a seat opposite the door and watched the young men who were obviously not waiting for a bus as they played the pinball machines situated in one corner, adjacent to a snack bar and a magazine-newspaper stand. One man who reminded Sally of Tim, one of the highschool kids who hung out in the game room in the back of the diner, caught her eye—she was trapped, she'd gone too far—and she watched him motion to his friend without making any attempt to disguise his gestures or what he was saying or who he was pointing at or *why* (though for Sally "why" could have meant anything: Why me?). She averted her eyes, but everywhere she looked there were people, strangers, whom she felt compelled to stare at. She had to learn how to look beyond people, or through them. If you looked at them directly it was necessary to pretend that you were thinking of something else at the same time, that you weren't really aware of what you

72

method was in the West Village, one medium-sized room with a kitchen built into one wall and a bathroom, filled with enough furniture left by a previous tenant so that if they wanted they could move in immediately. "Yes, we'll take it." There was no time to lose. The alarm rang at seven and Jacob was up, getting dressed, on his way out to look for a job. After weeks of inactivity they were suddenly overcome with things to do. Agnes spent half her day cleaning the apartment, the rest of her time checking the listings in the theatrical papers

---

were doing. If you looked too hard they thought you wanted something from them. It made them nervous, all except the young men in the terminal who thought, apparently, that being stared at by someone like her was funny. Everyone sitting down in the terminal appeared to be locked into gray pockets of anonymity, as if around the neck of each person there was a sign similar to the ones young married couples post on the doors of their hotelrooms: do not disturb. As always, there was the conflict between wanting to be alone and wanting someone to be there. If she was travelling with someone those guys at the pinball machine wouldn't dream of bothering her, and here they were now, smirking, surrounding her chair. No one except herself seemed bothered by their presence in the terminal, not even the policeman who lounged in the coffeeshop chatting with the cashier. I could get a job in a place like this and wait on all the young men with bleached hair who wander in off the streets, a waitress for lost waifs. Trying to pretend that no one was watching her (and no one was, really), she left her seat, bought a copy of Newsweek at the magazine stand, then crossed the threshold into the coffeeshop.

The stools had red upholstered cushions, just like at Price's. The lady in her late twenties behind the counter wore a white short sleeved uniform with the name Sara stitched on the pocket. Sally didn't feel hungry—she'd had a cup of coffee and a slice of toast before leaving the house—but when the waitress placed a napkin, knife and spoon on the counter in front of her she felt obligated to say something, though she barely trusted her voice, "I'd like a cup of coffee and one of those—" pointing to a random assortment of day-old donuts under a glass jar.

"Milk in your coffee?"

for auditions. Once they were settled they began taking turns going out separately at night so they could each have a chance to spend some time in the apartment alone. One night, on her way home from a play, Agnes was followed into the lobby of the building by two men who stole her pocketbook, and in her own words: "Could have raped me." (She was too embarrassed to tell Jacob what really happened, and somehow managed to get into the bathroom to change out of her clothes and rinse the taste of semen from her mouth,

---

The restaurant wasn't crowded, maybe every third seat was taken, but Sally felt guilty (overly empathetic) for providing more work for this thin-waisted Jane Eyre whose narrow arms floated freely in her stained uniform and who'd probably been on her feet since 6 A.M. She wished she was more adept at making conversation: the alternative was to forego that possibility or pretend the possibility of making contact didn't exist, and obey the mores of whatever setting you were in where people were too rushed to acknowledge what anyone else might be thinking or feeling. Pointless to expend energy on a relationship which you couldn't pursue past the half-hour you spent waiting for a bus to come, in a terminal where you've never been and would probably never return to: though the reverse of this was also true i.e. it was possible to condense intimacy into a few brief moments by conveying, and this was the doctor's secret, a sense of genuine understanding and sympathy. Most people think you're feeling sorry for them, "I don't need your sympathy, lady—I have two kids at home to support." Yet there was something intimate, not demeaning, about being served by another person. The finite number of people who entered the diner each day allowed Sally to relate to them all as individuals and she was quick to tell if their presence in the diner somehow related to their momentary need to be administered to in the simplest of ways. People would complain to her and she'd turn around and listen and watch their faces light up when she smiled. She could go through the motions of whatever she was doing, rinsing coffee cups or fixing milk shakes, without giving the person who was talking to her the impression that she was no longer listening. ("You'd make a good doctor yourself," Dr. Amundsen once told her.) Like the doctor, she could listen to people's problems all day. But learning how to get people to open

74

before he knew what was happening.) When she did speak her words echoed off the bare walls which seemed to shrink in around them as they sat on the edge of the bed ("here, drink this") which jutted out from one wall into the center of the single room, and a few days later they decided to move to what they imagined would be a "safer" neighborhood. Jacob, by this time, had found a full time job in the research department of a publishing company on Lower Park Avenue. They broke the lease on the first apartment and moved uptown, to

---

up and talk—that was the hard part, and in the city there were too many unknowns, too many variables, and anyone at any given time might question your motive ("do you really care about all this?") and turn off suddenly, mid-sentence. And if you just blurted out what was on your mind, oh well, she's probably crazy.

"Oh, sorry" some of the coffee had spilled over the side of the cup, it was the waitress's fault (may I call you Sara?), staining the front of Sally's dress. The last time I wore this dress what was I doing. "Take off your dress." "Here, help me with the zipper."

Sally patted the damp spot with the napkin and smiled at the waitress as if she—both of them—had just received invitations to a private party neither of them knew was being given in their honor, the anniversary of the occasion of the time they first met ("We met in a coffeeshop in Boston, 1980").

"Come with me—I'm going to New York—the next bus—"

If she were a man she might be permitted to say: "Meet me after work" or "When do you get off?"

(I had a husband too, if you must know, but he left me.)

Sally sipped her coffee and watched the waitress walk down the aisle to another customer, a bald business man in suit and tie, who placed his suitcase—as Sally had done—on the ledge beneath the counter. If she did stay in New York, as she planned, it would be necessary for her to begin her life over again—the clothing she brought with her wouldn't last long. Maybe, after a while, Bob would become reconciled to the idea that she wasn't returning and would pack all her belongings—her books, especially, and all the diaries and letters she'd saved from childhood—into a big carton and ship it all to her new address. She sank her teeth into the sugar-coated object the waitress had placed in front of her and swiveled slightly on the stool, the faces of three Cuban refugees staring at her from the glossy cover of the magazine she resisted opening but which she'd bought for moments when she had to pretend she was doing something else other than staring into space, or at the waitress who smiled back at her as their eyes met as if to say: I am free—say what you want—I'll go with you anywhere.

Sally turned towards the glass door of the coffeeshop and saw the same two young men, a tall blond twenty year old in tight dungarees and a rose colored cashmere sweater with nothing underneath and his friend who was older and swarthy with a blue bandana around his neck, whom she'd been watching before. They were standing at the door making animated animal gestures as if unable to decide whether they should enter the restaurant, maybe they didn't have enough money, when a third person brushed by them, a short man in his late thirties who reminded Sally of Pete (it was hard for her not to associate all the new faces with those most familiar to her: there were echoes and reflections everywhere), baggy army pants and a blue dungaree jacket catching his magical body like a deer on a mountain ledge or a wild dog in the Arctic leaping over the snow, he'd been moving forcefully, possibly he'd just stepped off a bus and was hurrying out into the morning streets to meet a friend or a lover or a wife when one of the two gazelles said something which made him break stride suddenly as if an arrow had pierced his side and in the same motion strike out with his fist, propelling it upwards into the face of the blond who at the moment of contact began to fall backwards against the window of the coffeeshop. As the man with the bandana reached into his pocket Sally's attention narrowed into one tiny frame where the only thing that existed was the reflection of the overhead beam of fluorescent on the point of the knifeblade that had emerged and was moving in an arc so quick the picture blurred as it passed through all the points in space in the universe before disappearing in a tangle of arms and legs, the bodies of the three men—now surrounded by other men and women leering over them—in a ragged pile on the terminal floor. The policeman and the cashier, this was happening on their turf after all and they didn't have time to be stunned, acted first, they couldn't just continue doing what they were doing or stand in place shouting "stop" or "help" or whatever word Sally had screamed aloud, unable to contain herself (and why should she, Bob was right, city life sucked, I'm going home). Except for Sally and Sara the restaurant

the top floor of a brownstone, just off Central Park, in the eighties. Months went by. This new apartment was so expensive it sometimes seemed that half of Jacob's paycheck was going to pay the rent. But after the "incident," as they referred to it, they rarely went out at night. For awhile Agnes had trouble sleeping and Jacob encouraged her to see a psychiatrist or at least make friends with the woman across the hall who had a young child but apparently no husband

---

was empty, coffeecups and half-eaten sandwiches—inedible anyway—abandoned in a long row on the counter. The crowd of people only moments before caught up in their own soap operas (I owe Herb $500 but I won't be able to pay him back until August etc) had been drawn as if by radar to the violent drama.

"You spilled your coffee again," Sara said, she was being Sally's mother.

The cup was empty, on its side in the middle of the saucer, while a brown fountain trickled down the edge, staining the hem of Sally's dress which Bob lifted over her head before cascading onto her suitcase. She remembered how shocked he'd been to discover she wasn't wearing anything else and in her naivete she'd thought maybe he's a virgin too and she knew it was because he knew she was a virgin and virgins at least wore underpants, right? Just like the girls in the magazine Pete was turning the pages there were coffee stains on her suitcase too and all life was reduced to simply refilling someone's cup, day after day. Here's a napkin. "Thanks—Sara." Patting the circles on her dress.

"I know that guy—his name is Gene—that's the blond—and the one with the knife, they're in here almost everyday. Just yesterday they were sitting right here, both of them, right here I mean and they'd just gotten money from somewhere, usually they pick up older guys, businessmen like the one who was sitting over there and go off with them to some hotel, you know. . . ."

She was talking not as a waitress but as a private person now, and in a quick bored monotone which made Sally think that what she'd just seen was a routine event on the city's agenda, tune in tomorrow for the great rape scene, same time same station. Not trusting her own voice, she could only stare back at the girl—wondering what she looked like without eye makeup or lipstick. Whether she was

and one afternoon when Jacob was at work Agnes convinced herself that she was being silly and overly self-conscious about just knocking on someone's door but when the door opened and her neighbor appeared still wearing her night-gown which it looked like she had just put on for the purpose of answering the door and Agnes could hear the voice of another woman in the background she backtracked immediately without even attempting to invite herself in. There was the possibility, as well, that she might be pregnant.

---

surprised or disturbed by what had happened she'd adjusted in a matter of moments—that guy outside wasn't her boyfriend or hus-band, after all, just another customer, and there were many custom-ers, many faces, new ones, different ones, everyday—and was tak-ing advantage of the break in activity to display some semblance of her off-duty personality.

"I knew there was going to be some action today—felt it, as I was going to work there was a fight in the train station and someone almost fell onto the tracks, accidents happen in groups you know like plane crashes." She could have been talking to anyone. "You from Boston?"

As she talked she stared through the window at the crowd, now mainly composed of policemen and people who worked in the ter-minal, the bystanders standing on tiptoe around the inner circle like a fringe on which a row of buttons had been stitched—eyes glazed and bloodshot from all the hours spent waiting for buses in terminals like this one, so even an act of violence—a stabbing, a murder, the sense that they were near death and in that way courting it (if only accidentally)—wasn't enough to give life to the vacant expressions on their faces. It wasn't quite the feeling of intimacy Sally had imagined, but now that they had shared this experience—and it was still continuing, she was still sitting at the lunch counter—there was still the chance something else would occur. In a few moments an ambulance would arrive, and a police van, and the three men would be taken away, the cashier return to his position behind the register, the business man to his abandoned plate of food—new people, who knew nothing of what had just happened, would push through the restaurant door and fill up the seats along the counter.

"Huntington? Sure I know that place. I have a sister in Concord."

Each morning, before he left for work, Jacob asked if she'd gotten her period. If she were pregnant they'd have to move to an even larger place (the new apartment had three rooms). When her period finally arrived it took her a day before she admitted it to Jacob, who pretended he was disappointed that they weren't going to have a baby, at least not right now. He didn't realize that Agnes knew he was pretending, and Agnes knew he didn't know. "He doesn't know what I want either," she thought to herself, in anger; it was the kind of

---

She scrawled a few numbers on her checkpad with a yellow pencil and handed the check to Sally, more out of habit—it was a gesture Sally recognized, she'd done it so often herself—than as a way of saying goodbye, in the formal sense. Sally wanted to tell the girl where to find her if she ever visited Huntington again—it was the equivalent of telling someone: here's my address, let's stay in touch—but as she searched her purse for loose change to pay for the coffee and donut she knew that the only time she'd ever see this girl was if she, Sally, returned to this bus station. She imagined herself coming back and standing at the window of the restaurant and pressing her face against the glass, waiting for the woman behind the counter to turn her way. Some people kept their jobs forever, others quit after a few months or were fired and collected unemployment, while some women—and men as well— regarded themselves as waitress or waiter, that was their identity, their profession, and worked their way up the steps of an imaginary hierarchy till they reached the small niche in life where they felt most comfortable about what they were doing.

"Did you see that? Did you see what happened?"

The cashier was a tall, overweight man, with broad shoulders— possibly, like Bob, an ex-athlete, whose career had been cut short by a freak accident—and short thinning hair swept back in an old fashioned pompadour. His cheeks were red from all the excitement and as he returned to his stool behind the cash register he loosened his tie and took a soiled handkerchief from the pocket of his linen sport jacket, wiping the perspiration from his forehead and eyes. His return to the restaurant was a signal to Sara that she had to resume her role as waitress or at least look like she was busy, even though there were still no customers in the coffeeshop except Sally. From a

blanket appraisal of everything that had happened to them since they left Boston. Their new schedule, along with the thoughts and fears of getting pregnant, had made them nervous about making love, "going all the way" as the girls in highschool, the girls Sally and Agnes had disdained, all of Bob Price's ex-girlfriends for that matter, called it. The more time they spent in bed, reading or eating or watching television, the less physical contact seemed to matter, as if actually

---

shelf behind the counter she took a damp cloth and began wiping the surface, emptying plates and cups into hidden receptacles and bins. When she was finished she circled back to where Sally was preparing to leave, all the while carrying on a conversation with the cashier (Sally noticed that they called each other by their first names), asking questions about what had just happened. At one point Sara looked up, surprised that Sally was still there ("can I get you anything else? more coffee?"), and Sally knew the spell had been broken by the presence of the third person. It was hard to keep moving. One of the reasons people stayed in one place for most of their lives was because of the energy necessary to propel oneself forward into a future about which they knew nothing. Just contemplating the unknown, as Sally was now doing, took energy, and a sense of perspective—when to save the energy, when to expend it—which Sally knew nothing about. Part of her wanted to sit at that lunch counter forever and hold on to some bit of knowledge which she had learned and which seemed as valuable as anything that had happened to her before. She wanted to digest the new experience before she was confronted by something else which she didn't understand. Her knowledge of herself had been limited to who she was in relation to her immediate environment, her life in Huntington, but now that she was no longer "Sally Price, waitress" she felt that there was some kind of gap which could be filled with almost anything, a tabula rasa, in the real sense of having no identity at all. She was a bridge between two points, the bridge was swaying in the wind, there was water below and boats and she was walking slowly with her old winter coat, collar turned up, wrapped tight around her shoulders while the people in the cars crossing the bridge passed her and looked out the car windows and honked their horns and shouted at her as if she was somehow intruding on some ideal

being part of the city had altered their metabolisms, and left them preoccupied, but not with one another. Each, in turn, began to superimpose characteristics of the people they saw everyday on the body of the person lying beside them, as a way of incorporating the collective psychic energy of the city without letting any specific person become a threat. Once every two or three weeks they took the subway back up to the Bronx to visit Jacob's father, and go with him to dinner at a

---

image, out for a country drive and there she was like a character in a poem by Wordsworth stumbling along. The cashier, and Sally too, and the blond prince whom the swarthy older man had punched and who in turn had possibly been stabbed by the third man who moved like a deer, were people whom Sally knew she would dream about or talk about to Agnes—they were part of her life now, part of the repertoire of stories, something she could relate to the person she was lying in bed with—and she couldn't imagine who that person was except she knew it wasn't Bob, Bob had been eliminated, someone else was sleeping beside him in her bed, in their bed, where she used to lie awake head propped against pillows and read till it was too late to even think he would come home (often he'd come home and find her asleep with the light on and the book still open, floating on the quilt). "Why should he come home anyway—he knows I won't sleep with him." She imagined herself sitting at a booth in a coffeeshop opposite Sara while a third woman served them. They were telling each other their life stories ("are you really interested?") and drinking coffee, iced, because it was the middle of summer and though the restaurant was air conditioned they'd been walking a long time hand in hand down an imaginary thoroughfare that reminded Sally of pictures she'd seen of Les Champs Élysées. Sara's shoulders were bare and Sally wanted to reach across the table and run her fingers through the girl's hair, but stopped herself and lit a cigarette instead. They were in a big city, New York, Boston, San Francisco—maybe they'd go visit Susan Amundsen who lived up the California coast with her supposed (ha ha) boyfriend. Agnes, it occurred to her, was probably as miserable as she was, so there was no reason why they all couldn't rent a car together and take off. Wouldn't that be fun?

local Chinese restaurant, and one weekend they took a bus to Huntington to see Agnes's mother, but otherwise they remained faithful to the pattern of streets and stores, subway entrances and neon signs, restaurants, luncheonettes and bars, hotel lobbies and offices, advertisements in newspapers and magazines, people in the street, parked cars, all the things they thought they might want to do and could never afford. Sunday was the best time to sleep late, linger over coffee, do The Times crossword puzzle, watch a ballgame, and enjoy the feeling of equanimity (if it was truly possible to enjoy being bored) which came from existing separately while still being together. Agnes stared at herself in the bathroom mirror for what seemed like hours, making faces at herself as she tried on new clothes, while Jacob, caught in a time warp of his own, puffed on a Camel at the kitchen table. He'd grown addicted to espresso coffee, Medaglia d'Oro or Bustelo, and bought a special pot which only made two cups at a time. On the radio Geza Anda was playing Rachmaninoff's Second Piano Concerto. Later they might take a subway ride to Battery Park, where everyone spoke a different language and carried a camera.

IT WAS COMMON KNOWLEDGE that no two people thought exactly alike. How could such a thing be possible? Everyone was imprisoned inside their own minds, had thoughts and memories meaningless to everyone but themselves. Occasionally, when two people who had lived together a long time found themselves reacting similarly to the same things, there were what might be thought of as "interactions." But mostly everyone just wandered around in their separate worlds, acting like monsters. It's also common knowledge that a body doesn't last forever. A lot depends (and I guess it's hard not to sound like someone's parent or doctor) on how careful you are as you grow older. When you're young it's easy to forget that your body is ever going to fall apart; you smoke, drink too much, take pills, and generally indulge yourself, thinking: why not? Any other kind of life that involves holding oneself back (and I'm not talking about a life based on ascetic principles) is like a kind of life-in-death, or so you tell yourself as a way of appeasing the mind inside your body. Do not worry yourself over what I'm doing you tell your mind as if it were a thing so separate from yourself you can actually carry on a detached conversation between a voice whom you think of as the voice in your head (your head speaking) and the other voice which is you, the person you really are. The mind holds the body at bay, at least for awhile. Then the body takes the controls, and you begin worrying: should I be doing this? Am I doing something wrong? People sometimes think of the body as a kind of machine. Bob once told Sally, trying to impress her, that the oil in a car was similar to the body's blood, that they both served the same function. Pete, who owned the garage across from the diner, had said the same thing, and Sally assumed it was the type of dumb statement men made in the company of women, assuming that women knew nothing about, say, cars. In Sally's case, alas, this was true. ("You don't know a fuck about anything," Bob would scream at her in the middle of an argument.) Pete lifted the hood to check the oil while her mind drifted off; now he was lecturing her about proper maintenance of this vehicle which she'd never wanted, could hardly drive. Sally noticed that Pete, who came into the diner everyday for coffee, was growing a mustache. They were inside the garage now, alone, it was afternoon, and Eddie White, the highschool senior who came to help out and "learn the ropes" hadn't arrived yet. This man could be saying anything to me, Sally thought, and she nodded, "anything you say," when Pete suggested leaving the car in the garage over night. "I'll have to ask my husband" might have been one method of postponing the issue, but the body does not work like a computer: I am not a machine. The engine might be compared to the human heart, and so on. Could you name all the animals that express emotions, noticeably, laugh and cry, actually shed visible tears? Sally knew Pete's wife, knew their daughter too. Everyone came into the diner, not everyday like Pete did, but for lunch, sometimes, or a cup of coffee. It was her body, but Pete owned the garage. Did automobiles have genders: fill her up? Maybe fill it up would be correct. He was in her blood (oil for blood was a trite comparison.) "Her blood ran thick like oil" etc. she'd heard that before. If Sally ever thought about what kind of men attracted her, she would have realized that Pete, the owner of the Amoco station in the center of Huntington, was no more her type than her husband Bob. (But who else could it be if not him?) In highschool Sally had written a paper entitled

"Women In Blue Collar Jobs" but she'd never contemplated getting a job in a gas station. Do you need any help? Every winter Pete hired a different highschool senior. "It's not like the old days when people stayed here in town; now they all get up and leave, even if it's for some other small town down the road." Oil, grease, tuneup, sparkplugs: these were not similes, or a secret code, a language like French which Sally and Agnes used to speak whenever they were in a crowd of people they didn't like. "Merde," Sally might whisper, giggling, "Merde alors." Who had taught them that? Did Pete know what they were saying? The idea of lubrication did have a definite sexual connotation. At least within the sexual vernacular the word could have a specific meaning. Sally wondered if there was a small room off the main work area with a sofa perhaps that opened out into a bed where Pete took women like herself ("you mean you'll do that instead of paying me for fixing your car?"), but she didn't notice any secret doors, only an alcove with a sink where Pete was standing, his back turned towards her as he tried to explain what was wrong with her car.

"WHAT ABOUT HER HUSBAND . . .
Is he coming too?" Jacob's voice was worse than any mugger.
Worse than the bicycle thieves who were referred to as
"rapists" by the newspapers when in truth all the girl had
suffered was a cut on her cheek and a bruised elbow. Worse
than the man who used to follow Agnes and Sally home from
rehearsals, who waited for them after school in the shadow of
a tree or the front seat of his car, and whom they called "The
Peeper" because once . . . (if you keep bothering me I'm
going to tell my mother).

Remember Babs LaRosa?

Looking for clues didn't prevent Jacob from being irasci-
ble. Words meant different things at different times. If you
wanted to make the relationship work you had to be careful
about what you said to the person you were with. Otherwise,
in the most simple-minded sense, misunderstandings (trying
to explain what you mean) would subvert energy better spent
attempting to get to know this other person. Mood
changes—when Agnes, for instance, was depressed, depres-
sions which could last for days—were most difficult for Jacob
to handle. He'd discovered that anything he could do in the
way of trying to get her to talk about what was wrong was
futile (phrases like "what's the matter?" only seemed to make
her feel worse), and that it was more important to be solici-
tous while remaining semi-invisible, be patient and let it ride.
His mind was elsewhere most of the time anyway; or possibly

he was depressed as well but just showed it differently. There was always the mass of language that got in the way of saying what you meant, of what was on the tip of your tongue at any given moment. Sometimes, when he returned home from work, he felt like an immigrant just off the boat or a migrant worker crossing the border, or that the person with whom he'd settled into life spoke a language that perhaps only a few rare tribes of primitive natives would understand. A confused band of signals, a grimace that really meant "I love it, I love *you*," a toss of the head that signified disapproval: I thought you wanted. . . .

Jacob took the stairs. It was raining. The lobby was empty. He didn't want to fight with her again.

"It's never what I want . . . it's always you. . . . It would be good for me to have someone come here for awhile. Tony stayed for two weeks and don't think that was any party for me. We never see anyone!"

Jacob remembered evenings in the Bronx when his father left the apartment mysteriously to go to the movies. Alone—as far as Jacob knew he and his mother rarely argued, or if they did it was when he wasn't around or when he was asleep and their argument took the form of a series of whispers or hisses, he went to the movies alone—or so Jacob's mother said—because he wanted to be alone, it helped him relax. Jacob sat in his room and studied. His father smoked a pipe, like Simenon. He pictured Agnes moving around the apartment, much in the same way his mother moved when his father left the house, clearing dishes, staring absentmindedly at the clock or her reflection in the window. Jacob and Agnes had played this scene only once or twice before: the first time, when they were living downtown, it had been an argument about moving again, and it was she who had actually packed a suitcase and gone out the door. Jacob stayed in the bedroom, in his familiar position in front of the television, watching a Yanks-Tigers game and reading a Nicholas Blake mystery simultaneously, wondering what his life would be like without her, if it came to that. Had she really gone?

Life wasn't a book you could skip through to find out what happened. There was no mystery, just a few facts that involved ways of being, attitudes, actions. A slide beneath a microscope on which you could observe your feelings reproducing and interacting. In the moment it was hard to know what one thought about or believed. The facts of the past always appear romantic compared to the present. When they first met Agnes had been more involved with the people and things around her than with herself, while Jacob had been more withdrawn, content to deal with the subtleties and facets of his own private world. Something would happen and he could sit back for hours, afterwards, drawing lines and connecting them to points in his head, creating ramifications out of tiny details. Replaying conversations: what people had said, what he had said or meant to have said. It was as if he were rehearsing for a play, while Agnes was already acting in it. For awhile, after they were first married, Jacob made an effort to engage his wife on what he thought of as "her own terms." He thought that becoming part of the other person, in some ideal sense, was what marriage—if this way of being with another person could be articulated at all—was all about. And Agnes, in turn, envied Jacob for having a world that wasn't dependent on anything external, not the weather or the war in the Mideast or the news of a plane crash in Miami, Florida. If he wanted to stay home at night that was fine with her, even if it meant feeling bored, restless—wondering if something was happening outside that she was missing. It was fascinating to be with someone who actually enjoyed being alone. "What are you thinking?" Agnes couldn't understand the purpose of having an inner world if you weren't going to share what you were thinking or feeling with at least one other person. She didn't understand "private" meant she was excluded as well. In Boston, where she knew a lot of people and had made a number of close friends during her three years at Emerson, there was always someone or something to distract her, but in New York, where she knew no one and it was dangerous to go out

89

alone—as she'd learned first hand—Agnes began to feel that Jacob had known before they moved here that their life would for the most part conform to the kind of life he wanted. Now he had her to himself. If he didn't want to go out, and he rarely did, then neither of them would go anywhere. He turned down the sound of the game and heard her footsteps, she was coming back, heard the door slam behind her, the rustling of clothing as she emptied her suitcase and refolded her sweaters and blouses into the bureau drawer. It was possible to pretend that nothing had happened. They'd move, if she wanted, but not tomorrow, or the next day. All one of them had to do was say something to evoke their past sense of familiarity and this hideous tension (which made them both feel like strangers inhabiting the space beneath a canopy in a storm) would end, would fade away. Tomorrow he would get up and go to work again, just like always, and when he returned home she'd be there in the tiny kitchen, he would ask her how she spent her day and he would make comments about what people he worked with had said, they might go for a walk or to the movies and as time went by they would make friends who would also be neighbors because that was the way things happened in the Darwinian sense of people banding together as units to preserve a tribe, even an artificial tribe whose common denominators consisted of books and records or occupations, shared interests, families with kids who had nothing in common meeting other families with kids the same age so the kids could play together while the adults, just the mothers usually, stood around talking about breastfeeding and tantrums and nursery schools, what their husbands did and maybe we should all get together some time, why not?

A woman in a fur coat stood under an awning on Central Park West while a doorman ran out into the street, his sleek turquoise raincoat flying out behind him like a French cape, the kind a schoolboy in a French movie might wear: *The 400 Blows, The Red Balloon.* Jacob walked through the rain, humming "Walk On By," heading downtown towards Columbus

Circle, Agnes and the apartment and the words that had passed between them dissolving behind him. Hard not to feel exultant at the momentary sense of freedom, even if it meant someone else was suffering. He'd find a restaurant that was open and drink a cup of coffee and then walk back and by then neither of them would even remember what they'd fought about. If that friend of Agnes wanted to come for a few days, that was O.K. with him, he'd made his point. Sally could visit and she and Agnes could go out together (there was some talk about "seeing a play") and he'd be alone for a change to do what he wanted. When he came home from work they'd be laughing at the dining room table, fresh flowers and a bottle of wine. Maybe dinner wouldn't be ready yet and they'd insist he come with them to some restaurant where there'd be no question of letting Sally pay for herself, not his wife's oldest friend who always acted like she was just waking up, a somnambulist, when he asked her a question it took her about an hour before she answered and by then he'd forgotten the question, he was just trying to make small talk, he was thinking about something else, his father in the Bronx, his mother in the kitchen, the girls at work, the book he was reading, Agnes would kick him under the table which meant "be polite" and which in another time would be more than a signal but an act of conspiracy or endearment which he would respond to either by smiling the benevolent smile of the animal who has just been fed or reciprocating by pressing down hard on her toe with the heel of his shoe so that she'd squirm momentarily in mock pain, making a grimace which meant, undoubtedly, "stop."

Pᴇᴛᴇ, ᴛʜᴇ ᴍᴇᴄʜᴀɴɪᴄ ᴀᴛ ᴛʜᴇ Amoco station opposite the diner, sat in his office turning the pages of a magazine, his attention stalled on a spread of color photographs featuring men in leather jackets perched on motorcycles, young girls in matching jackets unzipped to the waist sitting behind them, when Dr. Amundsen's car pulled into the station and stopped in front of one of the pumps. Babs and her baby girl sat in the front seat next to the doctor. Recently Pete had learned that his daughter Sandy was spending her afternoons in the game room at Price's Diner, and he was beginning to worry about her. She'd even quit the cheerleading squad and was talking about "leaving school," "moving to Concord," "getting a job." The freckles on the face of one of the girls in the cycle photos had reminded Pete of the afternoon last summer when he had taken his family to Laurel Lake, and where, after waking from a quick nap, he'd watched, squinting, as a girl in a yellow 2-piece bathing suit stepped out of the water and walked towards him, pausing at the lifeguard stand to chat and listen to the music that was coming from the lifeguard's portable radio. It wasn't until she was practically standing over him, water dripping from her suit onto his legs and chest, that he regained whatever sense of simple-minded clarity had been lost in sleep, and realized, saying the words out loud to himself: "that's my daughter."

Only last night his wife had told him the story about Babs LaRosa, and here she was, hardly a model of respectability and innocence, with the doctor no less. Pete bit his lip as he filled the tank, while Babs, who wasn't as pretty as Pete's daughter or any of the girls in the photographs, opened the door of the car, cradling her baby in a yellow sling. Though Pete pretended to be engrossed in his work, he had a heightened sense of awareness of all the people who passed through the station, and even had thoughts about them too: surmising, if they were strangers, where they were heading or where they were from. Each car that drove up was the source of a potential anecdote, something to talk about with his wife when he returned home from work.

"I saw that girl again, the one you were telling me about yesterday. . . ."

Babs, a shopping bag in one hand, the baby huddled against her breast, crossed the street and disappeared into Price's Diner. Dr. Amundsen asked Pete how his family was doing, the doctor had delivered both Sandy and Pete Jr., and with a little wave and a nod of his head as he signed his credit card, drove away. Pete signalled to Sammy, one of the high-

---

Now that Sally was gone Babs didn't care whether anyone in town found out about her relationship with Bob. Even if the woman came back after three days, wouldn't it be better for all concerned to clear the air of all the doubts and innuendos which had hung over their lives like morning fog for the past year? There'd been more than one occasion during the last month that she'd been on the verge of telling her mother, or the doctor, that Bob was the father of her child, but had held back, honoring Bob's request to keep his identity a secret. Babs didn't like being the third party, nor playing the role of catalyst in breaking up anyone's marriage, but from what she knew of Sally and Bob's marriage maybe it was just as well that it ended now, why prolong the misery any longer? And it was misery, hell on earth, no doubt about it. "Why, they don't even fuck!" she said aloud, staring at herself in the full length mirror on the inside door of the closet in the room in her mother's house. Connie had taken Mary for the afternoon and in a few minutes Babs was going to meet Bob

school seniors who worked for him in the afternoons, that he was going across the street for a break, and followed Babs, or at least the route she had taken. For all the hundreds of times he had been inside the diner, usually twice a day everyday six times a week, he'd never been in the game room.

Babs was sitting at the booth farthest from the door, her back to the door, nursing her baby. The diner was empty except for Bob, staring into space behind the counter, and a man Pete had never seen before who was drinking coffee and smoking a cigarette on the revolving stool near the cash register. The game room was located at the end of a hallway but first it was necessary to pass through a door in the back of the diner. Pete didn't know about the hallway. He thought the game room was right behind the door. There was no way to be inconspicuous about what he was planning to do, yet it was possible no one in the diner would even notice. He inched past the magazine rack, shuffling along with his eyes darting from floor to door to ceiling as if he were a prospective buyer (he'd heard a rumor that Bob was thinking of selling the place and moving to Canada), and when he reached the door glanced back over his shoulder to see if

---

at the diner. Living at home had its advantages, even though sleeping alone in her old childhood room made her feel like a young girl again. She fingered the buttons on her blouse, undoing the top one, and then one more, combing her red hair down over her shoulders. She imagined a time when she and Bob and the baby would all be living together, travelling in a van on the long highway that ran the length of Canada. The idea of moving to Canada had been placed in her mind by Bob and though it seemed a little remote to her (both the place and the idea) if that's where he wanted to go she was ready to follow. She could picture a house on the side street of the town where they'd be living, a town not much different from Huntington except that they wouldn't know anyone and no one would know them or what their previous lives had been like. Moving away from the place where one was born was like being reincarnated in one's own lifetime. Babs had no desire to let her reputation trail after her, like the hem of a long gown, forever. She wanted to take off the

anyone was watching. Babs, her blouse unbuttoned, was switching the baby from left breast to right. The sight of her bare skin triggered a chain reaction in Pete's mind which was already overworked and overpowered by the sudden train of associations in which the girls in the magazine and his own daughter and Babs herself were all superimposed on one another, arms and legs flashing obscenely, the same person intertwined. He felt that it was his duty as a father to see where his daughter spent most of her afternoons, and though he would have liked nothing better than to join Bob and the stranger at the counter his sense of the simple pleasures of life receded down a blind alleyway, dark as the hallway he stepped into when he opened the door.

For a moment Pete didn't know where he was. His first thought was that he had taken the wrong door. At the end of the hallway there was another door covered with a collage of photographs of rock n' roll and movie stars cut from magazines. Some of the faces were familiar to Pete since his daughter's own bedroom wall was covered with a similar display. Pete didn't like the idea that Sandy spent most of her time at home reading magazines bought, no doubt, at Price's,

---

gown and replace it with something better, something that fit. The bathroom scale read 125, same as she'd weighed before Mary was born, and though it pleased Babs that after almost a year and a half she could start wearing all her old pre-pregnancy clothes, she felt the need to draw a dividing line between past and present: the old clothes in her closet reminded her of some person she no longer wanted to be. "There she goes," she could hear their voices as she walked down the street. And she knew what they were thinking: who's the father of her child? The bathroom scale dipped back towards zero as she stepped off, bare feet on cold bathroom tiles. The house was empty, no baby crying behind a closed door in the middle of the night. It was unusual to have time to herself during the day. Her job, now that she was living with her mother again, was to wash dishes, do the laundry, clean the floors—all the household chores, but Connie was hardly strict about what had to be done when and usually the two women shared the duties—it was the one

but Pete's wife, wary of her husband's occasional bout of bad temper, tried to explain that their oldest child was just going through a phase, that all girls read those magazines and that it was just something girls do and that with Pete Jr. it would be the same only he would read different magazines, sport and adventure magazines like Pete himself read, and cut out photos of Fred Lynn and Dennis Eckersley and tape them to his bedroom wall, and that he should try to be more understanding, his children loved him, more patient. Sometimes Pete had trouble understanding just what he was supposed to do as a father, what was required of him, and it was the idea that he was finally making a move that gave him a momentary sense of purpose as well as the feeling that what he was doing was right, not only for himself and his daughter, but for a world that allowed men on motorcycles to ride through towns like Huntington and terrorize the young girls who didn't know better because their parents didn't have the time to spend with them or enough interest to find out what they were doing when they weren't home.

A baby was crying. It wasn't Sandy, "she's no longer a baby," Pete's wife whispered, not wanting Sandy to hear what her

---

activity they could really do together. A luxury just to be able to smoke a cigarette and stare at oneself in the mirror—turn, pose, posture, try on old clothes or new clothes, the little she had. As long as Bob remained married she couldn't expect him to buy her anything, not that he would even if he weren't married—he just wasn't the type to show up at her door with a basketfull of fresh flowers or a new nightgown: in fact he'd never even seen her in a nightgown (Mary had been conceived in the backseat of his car) nor had they ever spent a night together. A night followed by a leisurely morning over coffee at a kitchen table. When Connie and Babs cleaned house together, Mary sitting up in the playpen in the center of the livingroom, the older woman often confided in her daughter, and Babs wondered if her mother and the doctor would ever get together. From the way her mother talked it seemed more likely that she would be married before Babs herself, tie the knot so securely you couldn't pry it loose with your fingertips or the dull blade of a

father was saying about her, or what he'd do if he ever found her "with one of those guys" though who "those guys" were neither Sandy nor her mother nor Pete himself even knew. One reason Sandy spent so much time away from home was fear of how her father might react if she brought one of her boyfriends home. "I love daddy but sometimes I wish he'd just leave me alone."

The gameroom was more like someone's living room than one of the shooting galleries or penny arcades near Times Square which Pete frequented on his once-a-year trips to New York. There were no snot-nosed kids poised behind rifles aimed at moving targets, no pudgy men with aprons filled with nickels and dimes and quarters, no hustlers leaning forward from the shadows with eyes like frantic marbles sizing you up as you walked by. One of the two pinball machines, pressed up against the far wall of the room lit only by a blue bulb screwed into the ceiling, was out of order. Even the pool table was placed in a corner of the room, with just enough space between wall and table for the players to maneuver. An old sofa and some folding chairs filled an entire other wall. Only the jukebox, with a screen above the selection area which flashed different colors in time to the music,

---

rusty knife. One evening Bob met her (where's your wife? she was tempted to ask) in front of her house and they drove to a motel on the edge of another town about twenty miles away, and after the first time, with him lying back in bed wondering whether they should leave she stood up and did a little dance to the music in her head- –the kind of dance she did when she was alone, in front of the mirror – and that kept him there (that's the first time I ever did it twice, he admitted) for a long time afterwards so that they almost fell asleep in each other's arms. Then an imaginary alarm woke him to some sense or image of that woman lying in bed waiting for him to come home or maybe of his father and what he'd do to him if he ever found out he'd been sleeping with the so-called "town tramp." And maybe everyone knew anyway—Sally, the old man, etc.—and were too embarrassed or guilty about something in their own lives to blurt it out as a kind of reprimand which she'd heard half her life from the

drew attention to itself. If a slow song were playing, the colors merged at half-speed, reds and golds dissolving into misty blues. When a fast record was playing the colors vibrated, like a kaleidoscope. It was hard not to regard the machine as if it were a person suffering from synesthesia, and Bob often complained that all the colors gave him a headache. He didn't like fast songs, he was getting old before his time, and had tried to stock the jukebox with mostly slow records, to the consternation of the more recent generation of highschool kids for whom the diner had already worn out its usefulness and novelty as an after school hangout.

Except for Sandy and her boyfriend Tim, who were dancing in the corner near the pool table, the game room was empty. Pete recognized his daughter immediately, but his attention was diverted by the colors on the jukebox and by the song itself, an early recording by Elvis Presley which Pete remembered hearing years ago, when he was in the Navy. It amazed him that kids Sandy's age still listened to these same songs, as if nostalgia was a province reserved only for those who had reached middle-age, had something to look back on. "What do I have to look forward *to*," was Pete's constant mental complaint, shaped as a question from a self he was

---

voice in her own head which told her to stop hurting herself by giving pleasure, that it wasn't that easy and that there was more to being alive. The two months that she'd had her own apartment in Hopkinton, working as a waitress, had been the strangest time. Every night for a week she slipped the key to her apartment, which she kept on a ledge above the bar, into the pocket of whoever was left at the bar when it was time to close, a different guy every night. It was a short life and anything that would slow things down a little was a big help. She did a few situps and touched her toes with her fingers ten times. She told those guys to go to her room, and after the bar closed she'd climb the stairs and there they were, it was that simple, they'd always leave right after, go back to your wife and kids she hummed after them as she stared through the window which faced the street and listened to the engines of the cars turn over in the dead of night. And even Bob told her that when he stayed home with his wife on those boring nights after working all

only dimly aware of to the mirror image of a person he thought he knew but had trouble recognizing as he traced the lines and wrinkles extending from his mouth and eyes. Neither Sandy nor Tim were aware that he had come into the room. The boy's head was resting in the girl's hair, eyes shut, they swayed to the music, his hand on Sandy's back beneath her sweater which was raised slightly, her own hands knotted at his neck, almost on her toes so she could reach him while he bent forward to make it easier, head buried in shirt collar open at the neck. "Naked breasts against leather," Pete repeated the words as if he had written the captions for the photos in the magazine which only a few moments ago he'd been staring at in the office across the street. He recognized Tim, Pete played poker with his father and Tim himself had applied for a job at the gas station though Pete didn't remember his name. He wiped his hands on the front of his overalls and crossed the room to where the oblivious couple had begun bending backwards over the pool table, a final dip before the song ended. If Tim, not Sandy, had had his back to him it would have been easier to separate them, he could already hear his daughter's voice—"why don't you leave me alone!"—and what his wife would say later that night after Sandy told her version and was sent to bed and he and his wife sat at the kitchen table and she admonished him for

day in the diner, and they had dinner and possibly chatted about this or that and he would read the paper while she read a book or they both on rare occasions watched television though mainly it was he who watched while she read on the couch across from him with her legs pulled up as a kind of invitation to something that might happen later when one of them said I'm tired and the other kind of moved off to one side, and they followed each other up the stairs: even then nothing ever happened, she just rolled away, turned over onto her side, one night I got so mad I actually punched her (I mean she's my wife, right?) and the next day she showed up in the diner with a black eye. Next door neighbors in a small town can probably hear when two people are arguing without even listening. "It's just my body that I'm going to give him anyway so who cares?"

acting without consulting her first, they're just kids and it's best not to interfere (by now the whole town knows what happened), remember when we first met and we didn't know what my father would think, in a few years she'll probably thank you for what you did and Tim will too, she was trying to placate him while all he could do was nod his head and pretend that she was right, all the time knowing that she didn't know what he knew ("I saw that girl today, the one you were talking about last night, the one with the kid no one knows who the father is"—what was knowledge anyway but a combination of seeing and reacting and finally doing something about it all?) and that there was no way of ever telling her, or anyone, what was on his mind.

A SHORT WALK, JUST A FEW STEPS from the house to the bus depot. Do you have your ticket? She unzipped the narrow pocket of her bag and deposited the small cannister of pills beside her hairbrush and wallet. She had no fear, like Freud, of missing trains, only fear of change, even if the change was temporary, a 3 day visit—at least that's what she told Bob—to New York. The sound of the cup as it hit the tray like the crash of a child's cymbal was a sign that Bob was annoyed Sally, in her excitement, had forgotten the normal rules of diplomacy, wasn't even asking permission: "Agnes invited me . . . I'd like to go," but was telling him right down to the last detail of bus schedules and times what she was planning to do. For years he assumed that the only thing which divided their thoughts was a narrow membrane or connective tissue, invisible as the heart is invisible, and that this connection was like a web which surrounded them wherever they went, that it was there when they ate dinner together at the kitchen table where they were sitting now, or when they worked together behind the counter at the diner, or even, and this was the biggest delusion on his part, when they were in bed. She was already in bed, it was too early but he would join her anyway, sleep with her one last time before she left, just to make certain. . . . "Close the curtains." But if she wasn't going to be there tomorrow, what difference did it make now? Going away for

103

three days was a small intermission in the imaginary drama which he didn't know was happening since the only time he'd gone to a play (other than the highschool play Sally had directed) he'd fallen asleep with the program open on his knees. These days, the performers no longer wear clothing. The house lights went on. "Wake up son, it's time to leave." He was in bed but she wasn't with him anymore, it was only himself and the quarter moon behind the curtains, and the dirty diner where the kids came to play pinball and pool after class. Local basketball star hurts his knee. Sally sat on the side of the tub, brushing her teeth. Her thoughts were invincible; if she turned over on her side he'd come back to her and fill the empty space with thoughts that existed outside his mind. Tomorrow when she was gone, and he was free again, he'd turn into another person as well, the person he is when I'm not going anywhere, Sally thought, when I'm just here, the person who doesn't even bother coming home before three A.M. some nights and then he's drunk (she was rehearsing what she would tell Agnes when she saw her) and when I don't want to make love to him—and I don't, ever, I don't want to, at any rate—he goes downstairs and sleeps on the couch or makes me sleep on the couch: that's why I began ("see these bruises on my arm?") taking sleeping pills: the only person who knows anything about any of this is Dr. Amundsen. Split in two, it was possible for a person to crawl off and become the parts of themselves they were to begin with, and reproduce endlessly. "Demain" means tomorrow, or vice versa. We will now translate this news report into Spanish.

*

Sally hadn't gone to college because . . . there was no "because" in what she was trying to say. The bus was late. First Pete, from the gas station, waved to her from across the street, then Frank Myles, who managed the supermarket at the edge of town, drove by in his Stingray. How long would it take before everyone knew she'd gone to New York, that she'd left Bob permanently? If you stood in one place for an hour or two you would see everyone you knew, everyone who knew you by name, knew what your parents were like before you were born. And Dr. Amundsen, whom she hadn't seen or spoken to in weeks, would drive by along the road to Concord, and the sight of Sally waiting for the bus would make him think of his daughter and wonder what she was doing, waking up 3000 miles away in her house overlooking the Pacific. Or perhaps she was still asleep beside the "him" who was her husband. Perhaps she had taken a pill the night before when she couldn't sleep. So far from home, I know what you're thinking. That the reason I moved away was to get away from you. But you're wrong. ("I'm going to New York!") Bob had forgotten to shave; his beard, just the inno- cent hair that grew on his face, was too rough when he turned to kiss her, and she complained as she'd complained the first time they'd slept together, and he'd turned away thinking that if she really loved me she'd just endure the mild pain, engulfed in the sense of permission her presence beside him gave, guaranteed, in fact, like a machine filled with air and spirit. They would take a long bus ride together, at night, spread a blanket over their knees so no one would notice that she'd placed her hand down the front of his pants . . . at least that's what Bob thought when they were actually making love and he wanted to come. At least that's what Babs LaRosa, the doctor's daughter by proxy, would say, as he counted the buttons on her blouse when he poured her cof- fee, and she spun around on her stool everytime a stranger entered as if she were the receptionist or hostess and would approach this person who was just passing through town and wanted a cup of coffee and a slice of pie and with a sharp curtsy lead them or him or her to their table and when they were seated place foot long menus in their faces: would you like a cocktail— that would be one way to begin, spinning away from him as he reached forward, spilling the coffee he was serving her over blouse, skirt, bare knees. Bob's size allowed him to be as clumsy as he pleased, a bull in a chinashop, his height was like a deformity but he used it to advantage. If they sold the diner, if his father died, they could move to Canada, and start anew.

*

"Big fish, little stream." It wouldn't have surprised Agnes if Tony had made a pass at her. Jacob hadn't seen his brother in years, and Tony didn't attempt to hide the fact that for him, a stranger in the city, the family tie was just a matter of convenience, better sleeping over on someone's couch than spending money at a hotel or the Y. And soon he'd be leaving and they probably wouldn't see one another for 5 or 6 more years, and by then what had happened ("when does Jacob come home, anyway?") wouldn't matter.

"Agnes, I'd like you to meet my brother."

She watched the ripples begin to spread when the stone touched the surface. Then another stone, and more ripples, small brushstrokes in the painting Van Gogh made a few days before he died, crows flying over a wheatfield, she might go mad too and take her own life. It wasn't that serious only because *she* wasn't serious enough to suspend herself in space and allow her feelings to take over, to grow like shadows of boulders until she was pinned under by the weight. Watching the water move as the wind blew across the surface was good for her nerves (like taking a pill). She sat on the park bench and watched the bicyclists and all the single middleaged men and women wandering by with no where to go. If she could extend herself outward she would realize how much she was like them. Part of the past, part of the present, it all evens out in the end. The spokes of the bike turning beneath the cloudy sky, small comfort in naked branches. Move to a point, a place, an oasis, and stop and rest for awhile, breathe deeply and fasten your attention on an object cradled in space, rocking gently in the treetops outside your mind. Identify what you see. Don't stumble over your lines.

The Japanese teach their daughters how to make good wives. Serving is a pleasure. They bring you your tea, light your cigarettes. Serving is a form of power which the women exert over the men. Where would you be without me? The men are dependent on the women for domestic amenities.

*

It was Susan who had stumbled in with her cheerleading outfit and her batons to discover her father and Sally drinking tea together at the dining room table. "It's not as if I found them together in bed, or anything," she told her boyfriend, but the thought was in her head as a possibility nonetheless, and come to think of it worse things can happen, her father wasn't that old and since mom died I've been worried. . . . Hard not to think in clichés, like the time she and Sonny took mescaline and the phrase "Life is a bowl of cherries" reverberated through her brain, like a saying from The Upanishads, all the wisdom in those few sweet words. She placed the bowl of cherries between her legs and turned on the television. She could hear the buzz of water from the bathroom where Sonny was testing the shower. The erotic stillness of a bowl on a table, a bowl of fruit as a displaced symbol. "And later, without even telling them, he would make tapes of what they said, all those girls who came to see him with their problems. . . ."

Hi Dad, it's me. Sue.

The weight of one body on top of another. "I was going to write you, but I thought . . . well why not just call."

She placed the pits at the bottom of the bowl. After awhile, if she continued eating at the rate of two cherries a minute, there would be more pits than cherries. And then what would life be like, a bowl of pits? It was the rainy season in Northern California and the curtains billowed straight out like flags above a ballpark into the room. There was no moon. Most of her friends went to the diner after school but she went straight home, to get dinner ready for the doctor.

One day she came home and found Sally pouring tea for her father. Sally, who worked in the diner! Who was married to Bob Price, the former basketball star who still came to all the games. . . . "Huntington, Huntington, let's GO Huntington!" The male cheerleader, Ron, had his hands on her waist. It was a signal. In the air, flicking her baton towards the ceiling of the gym, she kicked her legs outwards and dropped; then he caught her again, as they'd practiced, breaking her fall. When her feet touched the floor she darted like a butterfly, a Monarch, to the sidelines. There were no more timeouts.

*

Jacob liked to read in bed. It wasn't unusual for him to come home from work, eat dinner with Agnes, and then—after coffee— "retire" to the bedroom. If he became bored with what he was reading, and he often read two or three books simultaneously to avoid this problem, all he had to do was reach forward and turn on the television. The image on the screen and the act of turning on the TV was like a flash of lightning in the distance, precursor to a summer storm, reminding him of his past and most notably his father whose first gesture of the day was to turn on the set which was connected in some way to a small mahogany platform which allowed him to shave and watch at the same time, the small screen reflecting his face. All relation between past and present occurred in a flash, in the time it took for the machine to warm up (so to speak).

"When's she coming?"

"She's taking the morning bus which means she'll get here— she'll come here straight from the station—when you're at work, but if there's any problem or delay she said she'd call."

On the TV a man with a mustache was flashing a stiletto in the face of a girl whom Agnes said reminded her of her sister Betsy, which was her way of saying that on this particular evening she was feeling sorry for herself, that she could identify with anyone in what she thought of as a predicament comparable to her own—for a moment all predicaments, or problems, were the same. It was possible that all she needed was someone other than Jacob to talk to, and if for no other reason she was looking forward to seeing Sally, even though in the past, in the unspeakable past, it had been Sally who had unburdened herself to Agnes, and wasn't that the reason why it was she who was visiting her? They sat on the steps of Agnes's mother's house comparing notes and telling stories. Highschool gossip. What do people talk about anyway?

"He gives the impression that he's being intimate, that he's revealing everything about his innermost life, while all he's really doing is telling secrets in order to cover up the real secrets."

Agnes guessed that it had been a flaw in her own personality that had allowed her to miss the genuine fragment of hypocrisy which was like a flirtation with death, a glancing blow, a stub on the toe, that seemed to shine like the vein in an old stone whenever she thought about Jacob, and which had come to dominate the part of their life which had previously enabled them to fit together into a whole section of a puzzle, that was life itself. Yet the map and the trails and all the missed signs which led somewhere only confused her when it came to point the way to the next plateau. She was here and most of the day he was over there, and when they were together he was still over there, seemingly all knowing, supercilious, as if the map were in his pocket and all she had to do was ask—beg for it— and he would unfold it, spread it out on the bed, and run a finger over the red line which led from point A to B and so on.

What was he seeing that she couldn't, that made him able to glide along? Not expressing what you were thinking made you seem stolid after awhile. What about the idea of "the long haul," of preparing for the future? Taking into account what you did today and seeing how everything you did fit into a plan you didn't know about but had meaning nonetheless?

The questions were audible, but she barely asked them of herself. She twisted the malachite ring he had bought her in Boston, long ago, when they would eat a breakfast of quiche and croissants, fresh orange juice and café au lait at an outdoor café near Harvard Square, spread a blanket on the bank of the Charles and watch the sailboats float by. Life was more than a metaphor, more than a memory, but everything could be turned around and adjusted to seem like something else, so that the water and the bank on which they sat and the boats themselves might fit into a larger picture, le Grand Jatte, an entity in itself, hard as rock, impenetrable.

*

Bob used the broom like a cane to propel himself up the narrow aisle behind the counter to where the stranger was sitting reading The Boston Globe over a cup of coffee. He'd taken a package of cigarettes from his jacket pocket and had placed it beside the glass ashtray, but wasn't smoking, waiting for the coffee to cool off. People who came in just for coffee usually smoked as well, so Bob had noticed. Or Sally had noticed and had remarked about it to him. Five minutes out of sight, and he was already off balance; five minutes after nine. He had told Babs to come in a few minutes before closing time, and now all he had to look forward to for the rest of the day was a visit from his father who would probably take Sally's departure as an excuse to berate him about the way he mismanaged the restaurant. If his father started in today Bob would tell him about his plan to sell the diner, even though he knew his father would probably blame Sally for putting the idea into his head.

At 10 Millie came on duty and Bob reminded himself to ask her if she could come in an hour earlier for the next few days; he'd forgotten to tell her that Sally would be gone. It was hard for him to put into words why she had gone (if someone asked what could he say?), hard to explain the unexplainable. If he did venture an explanation he would be

110

inviting the possibility of revealing something he didn't know about himself—or didn't know he was revealing—though that depended on who he was talking to, how much they knew about the situation.

Millie was laughing, his father was laughing, Frank Myles and Pete, the garage mechanic, chuckling to themselves as they went about their work, and even this stranger who'd never even seen Sally before would form an image of her in his mind when he heard the story, come to conclusions which reflected a version of the truth that arises when people are classified as types, taking nothing else into consideration (like all rapists are black, or so Bob's father thought).

Bob wished he could take a pill, like Sally did, she who had her reasons. A pill to make the day pass more quickly, or just blot it all out. This stranger was smoking now, and drinking his coffee, like a character in a play who took up space on stage, recited his lines and then exited—the way he came.

(Bob once had the idea of attaching a bell to the door in case no one was in the main part of the restaurant when someone came in but Sally vetoed the idea. "I'll go nuts if I have to listen to that bell ringing all day.")

FICTION COLLECTIVE
Books in Print

Flatiron Book Distributors Inc., 175 Fifth Avenue (Suite 814), NYC 10010